AMBUSH AT HOME

Nate started to step backward and aim the Hawken at the phantom figure, but his adversary was on him before he could squeeze the trigger. A heavy body slammed into his chest, knocking the wind out of him even as he was brutally smashed to the earth.

As Nate made a valiant effort to stand and resist the attackers, rough hands tore the Hawken from his hands. Other men seized his arms and held them fast while his pistols, knife, and tomahawk were stripped from him.

At the corner of the cabin a similar struggle was taking place. Zach was in the grip of three buckskin-clad Indians, who had taken his rifle and were trying to wrest his knife from him.

From inside the cabin, Winona shouted, "What has happened? Are you all right?"

"Stay in there and keep the door barred!" Nate said. "The Utes have us!"

The *Wilderness* series:

#16

WILDERNESS

BLOOD TRUCE

David Thompson

LEISURE BOOKS   **b**   NEW YORK CITY

Dedicated to Judy, Joshua, and Shane.
And to Beatrice Detwiler Robbins Bean. My mom.

A LEISURE BOOK®

June 2004

Published by

Dorchester Publishing Co., Inc.
200 Madison Avenue
New York, NY 10016

ISBN 0-8439-3525-1

The name "Leisure Books" and the stylized "L" with design are trademarks of Dorchester Publishing Co., Inc.

Printed in the United States of America.

Visit us on the web at www.dorchesterpub.com.

Prologue

From high out of the cloudy sky swooped a large golden eagle, wings outspread as it glided on the swift air currents always astir above the Rocky Mountains. Over jagged peaks and lofty cliffs it soared, seeking prey, its exceptionally keen eyes constantly roving over the rugged landscape below. Forested slopes unfolded underneath, the mighty pines appearing as mere bushes from the great predator's vantage point. Banking to the left, the eagle arced into a graceful dive that carried it to within a few hundred feet of the earth.

Now the golden eagle could distinguish objects the size of mice. It eagerly probed the high grass as it sailed across a meadow. Suddenly a flash of movement alerted it to a bounding rabbit which darted into the cover of a dense thicket. The eagle circled the thicket twice, saw there was no way it could penetrate to where the rabbit sat trembling in fright, and continued on its hungry way.

A steep mountain caused the scourge of the clouds to veer sharply higher, up and over a snow-tipped crown. Beyond lay a pristine valley. Thin columns of smoke spiraled heavenward from near a stream at the center. On spying them, the eagle tilted its wings to reduce its speed. Here was something new, something unexpected, and curiosity urged it lower. Caution, however, prompted the exact opposite a moment later when the wary bird detected a bustle of activity taking place among the strange nests made of buffalo hides from which the smoke wafted.

The eagle had seen such dwellings before. It had learned to associate them with the bizarre two-legged creatures who occasionally visited its domain. Once, when the eagle had been but a short while on its own, it had ventured close to a gathering of such creatures to better study them, and a small one had shot a slender wooden shaft that had clipped the eagle's wing and nearly brought it crashing down. Ever since the eagle knew to stay out of range.

Now the eagle observed dozens upon dozens of big and small creatures moving about and heard playful shouts and chanting. It noted the many horses and loud dogs. Bothered by the smoke and the noise, the eagle banked to the west to follow the stream out of the valley, and in doing so it discovered a second group of two-legged creatures in the trees bordering the strange nests.

This new group, the eagle noticed, was quite numerous. And they were moving quietly from pine to pine, making hardly any noise at all, so unlike the others. A little farther on, the eagle came to where many more horses were clustered together in a gully.

Changing direction yet again, the eagle was about to wing northward when its sharp ears heard a piercing shriek followed by harsh yells and a few popping retorts.

Puzzled as to the cause, it flew in a tight loop, back over the stream, and beheld a scene of sheer chaos.

The creatures who had been moving through the trees were swarming into the open and wreaking havoc among the nest dwellers. Figures grappled on the ground. Others fought upright. Thin shafts streaked every which way. Now and then one of the creatures would point a long branch at another and there would be a blast like thunder and a puff of smoke. There was much screaming and shouting.

Baffled by the bedlam, the eagle made a circuit of the site. Bodies littered the area. Some creatures were thrashing in torment or convulsing in the pangs of death. Pools of blood were everywhere, seeping into the earth.

The eagle witnessed countless brutal fights in which creatures were slain or maimed. It saw big ones ripped open by whooping foes and small ones who had their heads caved in. It had never beheld such outright carnage, such bloodthirsty slaughter, so it lingered, absorbing every detail. Its kind learned by studying other wildlife, by learning the rhythms of the woodland. It knew of the ferocity of grizzlies and the savagery of mountain lions, but it had never seen any sight to quite match this.

Since to the eagle all the two-legged creatures were more or less alike, it had no means to tell if the ones from the trees or the ones who lived in the conical nests were prevailing. It did see a shift in the conflict when dozens of creatures on horseback appeared over a hill and charged into the midst of the fray. Soon some of the creatures were fleeing into the trees. They raced to the horses hidden in the gully, climbed up, and swiftly departed. Many laughed and waved strips of hair.

The eagle made one final sweep. All the fighting had ceased, but some of the creatures were going around striking others sprawled on the ground if the latter showed the slightest hint of movement. Presently wailing and bawling arose, forming a mournful din that so upset the eagle it sailed off, heading deeper into the virgin wilderness where it could enjoy life undisturbed by the two-legged terrors.

Chapter One

Nate King raised his heavy ax overhead, then paused as the forest around him abruptly became eerily silent. Shifting, he scanned the nearest firs, then glanced at his prized Hawken rifle, which was propped against a convenient log. He had lived in the wild recesses of the majestic Rockies long enough to know that squirrels, sparrows, chipmunks, and the like only ceased their constant chatter when there was a meat-eater abroad—or man. Since the animals living close to his cabin were accustomed to his presence, he knew he wasn't the cause; there must be an unwanted visitor in the vicinity.

Lowering the ax, Nate stepped to the log and crouched. He strained his ears, but heard just the sighing of the wind and the rustling of limbs. Switching the ax for his rifle, he glided to the right and knelt at the base of a tree. The forest remained unnaturally silent. As yet, nothing out of the ordinary had showed itself.

Nate stayed perfectly still, his thumb resting on the cool hammer of his Hawken. His powerfully built frame was covered by fringed buckskins, his feet protected by moccasins. Perched on his head was a beaver hat, around his waist a wide leather belt. Wedged under that belt were two flintlocks, a matching set he had bought in St. Louis. Complementing the pistols was a big butcher knife on his right hip and a tomahawk on his left. In addition, he carried a bullet pouch and a powder horn, both slanted across his broad chest.

While Nate would have drawn stares back in New York City or elsewhere in the States, his attire was typical of the trappers and mountain men with whom he shared an abiding affection for the untamed but free life of the raw frontier. At the annual Rendezvous he wouldn't stand out of the crowd at all. And here, amidst the deep woods, he blended into the background so well that he seemed part and parcel of the forest itself.

Tense minutes went by. Nate had reason for concern—two very good ones, in fact—so he wasn't about to lower his guard until he was fully satisfied there was no danger. Foremost on his mind was the grizzly that had taken to paying his homestead regular visits in recent months. From the size of the tracks he had found, the beast had to be gargantuan. He feared it would one day attack his wife and children, and he wanted to end the monster's life beforehand.

Nate's second cause for worry lay in the Utes. He'd inherited his cabin from his Uncle Zeke, who years ago had built the sturdy structure on the northeastern fringe of Ute country. Since the tribe was notorious for driving off any and all intruders, the many attempts they had made to force first Zeke and now Nate to leave were to be expected. So far Nate had been able to repulse them, but one day, he often reflected, they might catch him by surprise and that would be the end of that.

Several more minutes went by as Nate's foreboding climbed. He gazed eastward, toward his home, dreading a scream or the boom of guns. The Utes might easily swing around him and pounce on his loved ones when Winona, Zach, and Evelyn least expected it.

A sparrow unexpectedly chirped, and was answered by some of its feathered fellows. To the southeast a squirrel began chattering. Somewhere a raven squawked. Whatever had upset them was gone.

The reassuring sounds brought Nate upright. He allowed himself to relax as he reclaimed his ax and scooped up the half-dozen logs he had chopped for the evening fire. Tucking them under his left arm, he hiked homeward.

All around him the Rockies were alive with movement and noise. It was early spring, when so many animals emerged from hibernation or shorter periods of forced confinement in their dens or burrows to revel in a renewed zest for life. Vegetation also thrived; the grass had turned from brown to green, leaf-bearing trees were adorned with buds, and flowers were growing once more, adding dashes of red or yellow or lavender to the brilliant strokes Nature painted the landscape with at this special time of year.

Nate wound along the game trail that connected the woodland to the lake situated east of his cabin. Underfoot were fresh elk tracks. Just a month previous, when heavy snow blanketed the mountains and wildlife was scarce, he would have been excited at the find. But now, with game again plentiful and a black-tailed buck hanging next to his horse pen, he merely noted the tracks for future reference.

Musical laughter brought a smile to Nate's lips. He turned from the trail, skirted some brush, and there was his cabin, bathed in the light of the afternoon sun. Even more resplendent was the beautiful Shoshone who stood just outside the open front door, her long raven tresses swaying in the breeze. In her left arm she cradled a tender infant, while in front of her frolicked a boy of ten and one other: a sinewy timber wolf marked by a white blaze on its chest.

The boy had a stick in his right hand and the wolf was trying to snatch it out. Spinning and twisting, the boy managed to keep one step ahead of the animal, which appeared to be enjoying the game as much as the youth.

"Try harder, Blaze!" the woman urged in flawless English. "Don't let Zach tease you!"

As if the wolf knew what she was saying, it suddenly clamped its iron jaws on the end of the stick and wrenched, tearing the trophy loose. Lips pulled back to expose its tapered teeth in a mischievous grin, it pranced rearward out of Zach's reach as the boy scrambled in pursuit and the mother laughed harder.

"I thought the two of you were going to skin the buck, Winona," Nate pretended to chide as he approached. "But look at this. I leave for a little while and the two of you act the fool."

Winona looked up, smirking, and countered by saying, "Your people would be better off, dear husband, if they knew how to enjoy themselves more. Whites are too serious for their own good."

Nate thought of the hectic pace of life in distant New York City, where he had been born and raised, and frowned. He recalled having to get up before dawn every morning to trudge to his boring job as an apprentice accountant, where he spent his days laboring over heavy books packed with scribbled figures, toiling until well past dusk in many instances in order to complete the work that needed doing. Then he had trudged home, gulped his supper, and had to spend an hour or two doing chores around his parents' house. By the time he crawled under the covers, he was exhausted. On his only day off of the week, Sundays, there had been church to attend and endless visits to relatives and friends. Seldom had he been privileged with time to himself to spend as he saw fit.

Now that Nate gave the matter some thought, he realized he did have much more free time since coming to the mountains. In a way, his life in the Rockies reminded him of the carefree days of his early childhood, before his schooling years began. Here, at least, he was often able to do the things he *liked* doing rather than being a perpetual slave to things he *must* do.

Indians were the same way. They rarely rushed anywhere. They never hurried to complete work, and never crammed their days with so many activities they had no time to themselves. They lived day to day, hand to mouth, handling whatever came up as it arose, yet they were invariably happier and healthier than their white counterparts who toiled endlessly at sheer drudgery. Ironically, it was the whites who considered themselves superior because they were civilized; the Indians were simple savages who knew nothing about life.

"I won't argue with you there," Nate conceded, and gave his wife a peck on the cheek. "Though with that mangy grizzly hanging around, I don't figure it's wise to let the buck hang out overnight. The bear's likely to pick up the scent and pay us a call."

"Is the mighty Grizzly Killer afraid of one bear?" Winona taunted, referring to him by his Indian name. "I thought you have only to look at a grizzly and it drops dead at your feet."

"If only it was that simple," Nate muttered. He had tangled with the fierce brutes on a half-dozen occasions and he had no wish to ever do so again. As Meriwether Lewis, one of the leaders of the famous Lewis and Clark expedition, had often said, grizzlies were incredibly "hard to die." They were almost indestructible, as many a trapper had found out to his fatal dismay. A single ball to the brain or heart seldom sufficed. Usually, they kept on charging after being shot repeatedly, and even though mortally wounded, would rip whoever had shot them to shreds before expiring.

Turning, Nate took the wood inside and stacked the logs next to the stone fireplace he had built with his own two hands. The ax went in a corner. Then, drawing his knife, he went out, and was pleased to see his wife and son already at the carcass. Little Evelyn was propped in her cradleboard against the side of the cabin, Blaze at her feet.

Several of the horses had gathered at the rails to watch, among them the large black stallion Nate liked. He stopped to stroke its neck and scratch behind its ears, saying, "I know you've been cooped up for quite a spell. But I'll take you for a ride soon. I promise."

"Can we all go, Pa?" Zach piped up. "I was sort of hoping we could pay Uncle Shakespeare a visit."

Nate smiled at the notion. Shakespeare McNair was no blood kin of his, but the two were the best of friends. More than that, Nate loved the grizzled mountain man like a second father. It was McNair who had served as his mentor after the death of his uncle, and now the two of them invariably traveled and trapped together. "I like that idea," he declared. "It's been three or four moons since we last saw him."

"And Blue Water Woman," Winona said, alluding to McNair's Flathead wife. "She and I will have much gossip to share."

"Just so none of it is about me," Nate commented, moving to the buck. "The two of you have the darnedest knack for telling tales out of school."

"Can I help it if husbands are such a wonderful source of humor?" Winona responded. "Men so love to bluster and swell their chests all the time, yet at heart they are like young boys. And they do just as many silly things."

"Is that true, Pa?" Zach asked.

"Pay her no mind, son," Nate said, facing the belly of the deer. "Everyone knows how contrary females can be." Gripping a foreleg, he inserted the tip of his razor-sharp blade and proceeded to make a slit down the middle of the belly, from the chin to the tail. Since he wanted to save the hide, he cut carefully, making the opening as straight as he could. Next he sliced down the inside of the front and hind legs, starting at the knee joints. He avoided touching the scent glands since bucks often urinated on them during the rutting season and he didn't care to accidentally contaminate the meat. For the same reason he severed the esophagus close to the head and tied a whang around it to keep the contents from spilling out. Likewise with the anus.

The intestines Nate saved. Back in New York he would have thrown them out because they were regarded as unfit to eat, but he had learned long ago that Indians ate them regularly, and in fact he had acquired a taste for them himself. He chopped off a portion and tossed it to Blaze, who snatched the morsel up and moved into the brush to feast undisturbed.

Winona and Zach were doing their share of the labor. While the boy removed the meatless lower legs by cutting into the cartilage and ligaments and then twisting, Winona took out the heart and liver. She grinned at Nate, then bit into the raw heart, heedless of the rivulets of blood that streaked her chin and neck. Chewing lustily, she offered it to him.

"Thanks," Nate said, and took a bite himself. He savored the warm meat, the tangy taste of the blood, reflecting that if his childhood friends could see him now, they'd likely recoil in shock at his barbaric behavior.

The remainder of the afternoon was spent cutting most of the meat into thin strips which were hung over a crude wooden frame Winona constructed. Several sizeable steaks were placed inside for their supper. Blaze was treated to odds and ends, and by evening was contentedly full.

Winona submerged the hide in a basin of water. When, eventually, the hair slipped off, she would pull and chew the wet hide until it was suitably supple. To further soften it, she would then apply a paste made from the animal's brains into the hair side of the skin. By the time she was done, she would have excellent buckskin to use in the making of a shirt, leggings, or whatever else she desired.

Twilight was nipping at the countryside when Nate led his loved ones down to the lake where they could wash up. His hands and forearms were spattered with blood and gore up to the elbows, so he plunged both into the cold water and swirled them around. Out on the lake ducks, geese, and gulls were settling down for the night. He saw several concentric ripples caused by fish surfacing, and spied a large one that leaped clear out of the water, then smacked down with a loud splash.

As Nate rose, he inhaled the crisp, invigorating air and admired the magnificent ring of mountains surrounding his secluded valley. To the south was the highest, named after an army major who had explored the territory not too many years earlier: Long's Peak. It dominated the region, serving as a landmark for whites and Indians alike. At the moment, with its white cap of snow set ablaze in striking hues by the dazzling setting sun, it resembled a volcano about to explode.

Was it any wonder, Nate asked himself, that he so loved the Rockies? Untamed, formidable, stately monarchs that they were, the mountains brought out the best in men and women by challenging those who would live among them to struggle to simply stay alive. Such hardship, he had learned to his surprise, had the capacity to hone a person as a whetstone honed a hunting knife. It had actually made him stronger than he ever thought he could be, and for that he would be forever grateful.

Sometimes Nate shuddered when he pondered how his life would have turned out had he stayed in New York City. He would no doubt be flabby and lazy, so softened by easy city living that he couldn't walk more than a mile or two without being winded. He would be dependent on others for his food and clothing, unable to fend for himself even if his life depended on it. That was what civilization did to a man. It turned him into a pale shadow of his natural self, into a pitiful imitation of the hardy, independent soul he was meant to be. Thank God, Nate mused, he had come West!

Pivoting, Nate surveyed the forest beyond his cabin. A red hawk was winging its way northward. He studied it to see if it would abruptly turn off course or give some other indication of spotting something unusual below, but it never did. Rolling down his sleeves, he hitched at his belt, adjusted his flintlocks, and with one arm over his wife's shoulders and another over his son's, he headed up the trail.

"Are we going to the Rendezvous this summer, Pa?" Zach casually inquired.

"We are if we haven't gone under. Why?"

"Well, you know I have a few plews of my own to trade for whatever I want."

"And fine pelts they are," Nate commented. "You did real fine catching those beaver all by yourself."

Zach beamed with pride. "Do you figure I might be able to trade them for a pistol of my own?" he asked, and went on quickly to justify his request. "Ma has one. You have two. But I don't have any, and you told me once that I could when I was old enough. I think I'm old enough right now."

"You do, do you?"

"Yes, sir. And since I'll be off hunting and whatnot by my lonesome now and then, I figure I need a gun in case I run into trouble."

Winona, who had been cooing softly to Evelyn, glanced around. "I agree with him, husband. Shoshone boys his age have their own bows and lances. It is fitting he have a pistol."

"How can this coon say no? I reckon I'm outnumbered," Nate joked. In truth, he would have agreed anyway. A pistol was an indispensable tool for anyone who wanted to last long in the wilderness, the same as a rifle or a knife. Depriving his son of either might mean the difference between life and death for the boy.

Blaze had disappeared when they reached the cabin. Of late the wolf had developed the habit of running with its own kind at night and returning to the cabin to rest up during the day.

Nate and Zach buried the remains of the buck so the scent of blood wouldn't attract unwanted company. They checked the corral, made a circuit of the cabin, and entered to the tantalizing aroma of roasting steaks. Nate barred the door, set his rifle by the jamb, and gratefully sank into the rocker positioned near the fireplace.

This was the quiet hour of the day Nate so enjoyed. He broke out his pipe, stuffed the bowl with kinnikinnik, and settled back to smoke and plan. In another week or so he would be leaving to set his spring trap line. By rights he should have headed out two weeks ago, but he had been reluctant to leave his family, to give up the tranquility of his home for the harsh demands of the forest. The thought made him chuckle. City living, apparently, wasn't the only kind that made a man soft.

Winona hummed as she prepared their supper. Zach was poring over a book at the table. The scent of burning pine filled the cabin, and the crackling of the dancing flames added a comforting note.

Drowsiness overcame Nate. He daydreamed about the last Rendezvous, where he had won a fine new Hudson's Bay three-point blanket in a wrestling match with a rowdy Canadian. The man had been as strong as an ox, and only by a sheer fluke had Nate prevailed. He remembered the startled look on Rene's face, the cheers of the onlookers, and the—

"Pa?"

Nate blinked and roused himself. "What is it?" he replied, lowering the pipe. "Time to eat?"

"No. Didn't you hear the horses?"

Straightening, Nate cocked his head and listened. "Afraid not," he admitted. "What were they doing?"

"Acting up," Winona answered. She was staring at the sole window, which ordinarily was covered by a leather flap that earlier she had tied at the top to admit fresh air. "Perhaps the grizzly is around again."

"I'll go have a look-see," Nate sighed, placing his pipe on the shelf rimming the hearth. He loosened his pistols on the way to the door.

"Can I come too?" Zach asked excitedly.

"You stay with your mother and sister," Nate advised.

"Ahhh, Pa."

"What if it is a grizzly and it gets past me?" Nate mentioned. "Have your rifle ready just in case." Removing the bar, he held the Hawken in his right hand, then worked the latch and swiftly slipped out, pressing his back to the wall so nothing could get at him from behind. Night reined, and the woods bordering his homestead were inky black. The lake appeared as a slightly paler blotch against the backdrop of shadows. Nothing stirred anywhere. There were no sounds other than the wind.

He pulled the door shut, crouched, and worked his way to the corner.

All the horses were congregated at the southwest corner of the pen, the stallion at the front with its head high, ears pricked, and nostrils flaring.

Nate knew the animals had scented or seen something prowling about in the pines. Easing onto his stomach, he began crawling around the corral, never losing his grip on the Hawken for an instant. Taking his cue from the stock, he guessed that whatever had them so agitated was due south of the cabin.

In the woods a twig snapped.

Freezing, Nate scoured the gloom veiling the trees for evidence of the intruder. Whatever was out there had stopped moving or else was being as silent as a ghost. He snaked to the end of the rails and peeked around them.

Rising to his knees, Nate leaned against the post, biding his time, waiting for the nocturnal prowler to give itself away. He had a long wait. Over ten minutes went by, and then, to the west, there was a muted thud. Perplexed, Nate rose until he could see over the pen. He wasn't quite certain if one of the horses had stamped a hoof or if something else had been responsible.

Taking a chance, Nate ventured around the bend, moving further and further from the cabin and sanctuary. He remembered to cock the Hawken, and did so with his other hand covering the hammer to muffle the metallic click. As he came abreast of the horses, the stallion nickered, as if in warning.

In the distance a coyote yipped and was answered by another. In the depths of the woods an owl hooted. Something else screeched.

Nate reached the southwest corner and halted. He hugged the post, relying on its squat shape to distort his silhouette. Again he waited, exercising patience a panther would have envied. He heard the plaintive howl of a lonely wolf, but that was all. When close to 15 minutes had elapsed and there had been no sign of man or beast, he shifted position, stealthily padding to the rear of the cabin. Here, where the murk hung thickest, he was invisible to prying eyes. He let another 15 minutes go by before concluding he was expending all this effort in vain. If there had been a bear nearby, it had decided to go elsewhere.

Relieved, Nate stood and walked along the wall to the northwest corner. The wind struck him full in the face, fanning his shoulder-length hair and beard. He pulled his beaver hat down and kept on going.

On this side of the cabin stood an ancient spruce. During the hot months it provided welcome shade, and under its spreading branches the family often sat and chatted when there was no work to be done and the weather was fine.

Nate felt something brush his cheek as he passed the wide trunk. Reaching out, he found the rope he had tied to a low branch the previous year for Zach to swing on. He gave it a shove, then took another step.

A bright square of light suddenly appeared in the trees fronting the cabin, a lean shadow framed at its center.

"Pa?"

"Around here," Nate answered. The rope grazed his head again as the square of light blinked out simultaneously with the slamming of the door. He saw Zach stride into view. "Something wrong, son?"

"Ma was getting worried, is all. She sent me to find you. Is everything all right?"

"As peaceful as a church service," Nate said.

"What had the horses spooked?"

"Your guess would be as good as mine. Those fool horses act up if a mouse farts."

The boy burst into hearty laughter. "You're lucky Ma didn't hear you say that. She's a stickler for polite talk."

"Which has never failed to tickle my funny bone," Nate admitted. "Somehow I figured she'd be different, what with her being Shoshone and all." He idly scratched his chin. "Let that be a lesson to you. Women are women, no matter what color their skin happens to be."

"Is that important?"

"You'll think so when you're older," Nate said. Once more the rope swung against him, and he wondered why it was still moving when he had only given it a light push. Glancing upward, he was shocked to behold a squat black form balanced on the limb to which the rope was tied. At that very instant, the form sprang.

Chapter Two

Nate reacted as swiftly as anyone could. He started to step backward and to aim the Hawken at the phantom figure, but his adversary was on him before he could squeeze the trigger. A heavy body slammed into his chest, knocking the wind out of him even as he was brutally smashed to the earth. In a daze, he heard his son cry out, then the blast of Zach's rifle. Dimly he became aware of other figures pouring from every direction.

If there is any one moment in a man's life when he will disregard personal danger and refuse to bow to basic animal fear, that moment is when his family is threatened. The instant Nate perceived that his loved ones were at grave risk, he shook off the effect of the blow and made a valiant effort to stand and resist the attackers. But his effort was too little, too late. Rough hands tore the Hawken from his hands. Other men seized his arms and held them fast while his pistols, knife, and tomahawk were stripped from him.

At the corner of the cabin a similar struggle was tak-ing place. Zach was in the grip of three buckskin-clad Indians who had taken his rifle and were trying to wrest his knife from him.

"No!" Nate roared, redoubling his attempt to break free as four warriors hauled him upright. The grip on his right arm slackened a bit, and with a savage wrench he tore it loose and drove his fist into the brave in front of him, causing the man to stagger rearward. Twisting, Nate connected with a second chin, which freed his left arm.

Like a vengeful whirlwind Nate tore into the remain-ing pair, his large knuckles splitting their cheeks and battering their brows. One of his punches struck a mouth and there was a distinct crunch. Momentarily in the open, Nate whirled and raced to his son's aid. Zach was on the ground, a brawny warrior astride his chest. The other two had vanished.

In a single long stride Nate drew abreast of the brave on Zach just as the man turned to see how his compan-ions were faring. Sweeping back his leg, Nate planted his foot squarely in the warrior's face, catapulting the man into the grass. He lunged down, grabbed the front of Zach's shirt, and swept the boy to his feet.

Nate barreled toward the front door, but he'd only taken a few steps when he saw the gathering of dark shapes outside it and heard them battering at the wood to gain entry. Pure rage pumped through his veins as he thought of the fate awaiting his wife and daughter if the hostiles were successful. Letting go of Zach, he took a flying leap and plowed into the group, scattering them like leaves before a gale.

But the tide of battle quickly turned. Nate landed hard on his elbows and knees. He began to push upright when five or six warriors swarmed on him at once. Their com-bined weight was too much to resist. They flattened him, pinning him helplessly as his arms were clamped in grips of iron. Frustration combined with anxiety for his family to drive him into a frenzy, yet no matter how hard he tugged and thrashed he was unable to throw the warriors off.

From inside the cabin, Winona shouted in Shoshone, "Nate? Zach? What is happening? Are you all right?"

"Stay in there and keep the door barred!" Nate said. Looking up as he was lifted to his feet, he got a good look at a brave in front of him and a chill rippled down his spine. "The Utes have us!" he added, trying to keep his voice level and calm. The moment he had long dreaded had finally arrived, he thought bitterly. His enemies had him in their clutches. He was completely at their mercy, the outcome inevitable. They would torture him, slowly, so he died a horrible, lingering death. Worse, they would do the same to Zach, then either kill Winona and Evelyn or else adopt them into the tribe, and there was nothing he could do to prevent it. Despair replaced his rage, but he stood with his shoulders squared, his head held high, determined not to show any weakness.

More warriors were joining those near the door. A pair held Zach between them. The boy was doing his best to imitate Nate's example. His voice, though, wavered when he asked, "What now, Pa? Will they kill us right off?"

"I don't rightly know," Nate hedged. He saw some of the braves gazing at the forest as if they were expecting someone, and sure enough a lone warrior shortly appeared. A husky, muscular man with flowing black hair, he strode across the open space and halted right in front of Nate.

"We meet again, Grizzly Killer," the Ute remarked in sign language, moving his hands slowly so his gestures would be easy to read in the dark. "It has been many moons."

Nate's astonishment must have been obvious because the tall warrior laughed. "Two Owls," Nate murmured aloud in English, forgetting himself. He did indeed know this warrior; Two Owls was a Ute chief whom he had briefly befriended over eight years ago. The two of them had paired up to drive off a Blackfoot war party, then gone their separate ways, and he hadn't seen the man since.

"We have come in peace," the Ute now signed. At a spoken command in his own tongue, those restraining Nate and Zach released their holds and stepped back.

"You have a strange way of showing it," Nate signed in response.

"Here is proof," Two Owls said, and again he reverted to the Ute language.

Nate was flabbergasted when all of his weapons were promptly handed over, as were his son's. He accepted them silently and regarded his former acquaintance with interest.

"I am here to talk about a matter of great importance to both of us," Two Owls went on. "I apologize for the way we have treated you, but I could not be sure what kind of reception we would receive. It is said you shoot Utes on sight."

"You cannot blame me," Nate responded. "Every Ute I have ever met except for you has tried to take my hair."

Two Owls frowned. "The other chiefs do not think as highly of you as I do. Long ago I told my people of the service you did us and asked them to let you live here in peace. They accepted my words, and none of my warriors have ever bothered you." He gave a shrug. "But those from other villages do not see you as a friend. I have heard of the many attempts they have made to put you under. For this I am very sorry."

The chief's sincerity was self-evident. Nate cracked a lopsided grin, then signed, "Perhaps you should call a council of all the chiefs so I can present my request to be left alone in person."

"There are a few who would kill you the moment they laid eyes on you," Two Owls replied. "But I do have an idea how you can change their thinking." He nodded at the cabin. "If you invite me into your strange wood lodge, I will explain."

Nate glanced at the ring of warriors, debating the wisdom of having Winona open the door with all of them there. Suddenly he realized that none of the braves were armed, not even with so much as a knife, a fact he had overlooked before in the rush of events. He commented as much to Two Owls.

"Yes. I had every member of my band put all his weapons down before we moved in because I did not want you to be accidentally harmed." The chief addressed his men, and like ghostly specters every last one melted into the shadows. "I want you to feel safe, so I have told them to wait in the pines until I call."

"You think of everything," Nate complimented him. Any lingering doubts he had entertained were gone. He had turned toward the door to knock and inform Winona that all was well when the door swept inward to reveal her holding a cocked pistol in one hand and a tomahawk in the other. In a flash he discerned her intention from the fiery expression she wore, and he leaped forward to swat the pistol upward just as she extended her arm to shoot. "Don't!" he declared. "Everything is fine."

Winona glanced at him in confusion. "It is?"

"The Utes are friendly," Nate disclosed, giving her a reassuring smile.

"But the shot? And the fighting I heard? And you said—"

"I know what I said, but I was wrong." Nate indicated the chief. "This is Two Owls."

"The one you told me about long ago?"

"The very same."

Although Winona was clearly bewildered, she had the presence of mind to compose herself, lower the pistol, and step aside so they could enter. She stared suspiciously at the chief, and once the door had been barred and Nate and Two Owls were seated at the table, it was noteworthy that she kept the pistol close at hand at all times.

Nate had taken a seat facing the door and window. He offered the Ute coffee, and while Winona brought over two tin cups he got to the point by signing, "So what brings you so far from your people?"

"Have you ever heard of Bow Valley?" Two Owls rejoined.

"No."

"Has your woman?"

Shifting in his seat to inquire, Nate found her watching them intently.

"Every Shoshone knows of it," she answered. "Bow Valley is where my people have gone for more winters than anyone can remember to obtain the best wood there is for making bows. Our warriors say such wood never breaks or warps. Bows from there are considered good medicine and every man wants one."

"What kind of wood do they use?" Nate probed in English.

"I believe whites call it ash."

"Bow Valley is a special place for my people too," Two Owls signed after they were done speaking and Nate had signed Winona's reply. "It is where we go not only to make bows but to commune with the Great Mystery and hold dances. Like the Shoshones, we have been doing this for longer than any man can remember."

"It must be some valley," Nate observed to be polite.

"There was a time when the Utes and the Shoshones shared it," Two Owls disclosed. "The Shoshones liked to come during the Crow and Grass Moons, while my people preferred to go there during the Heat and Thunder Moons. There was never any problem because the valley was considered neutral territory and neither tribe was ever there at the same time as the other."

"But something changed?" Nate asked.

Two Owls placed his hands on the table and folded his hands. "Many winters ago two parties came to the valley on the same day. The Utes were led by Bear-Loves, the Shoshones by a warrior named Dry Eyes. They argued, each demanding the other leave. Soon they came to blows and the warriors from both sides fell on one another. There was a great fight. Many coups were counted. Many braves died. One of them was Bear-Loves himself." He gazed at Winona. "Do I speak with a straight tongue?" he signed. "Is this not the way it was?"

"Yes," she answered.

"Ever since," Two Owls continued, "our two tribes have fought over the valley. If the Shoshones find Utes camped there, they attack. If my people discover Shoshones camped there, we attack. Many, many lives have been lost."

There was a note of sadness in the chief's tone that sparked Nate to inquire, "Have you lost someone close to you because of this conflict?"

"Yes. One moon ago two of my cousins, Chased-by-Hawks and Short Lance, took part in a raid on a Shoshone camp. Both were slain. Their bodies were never recovered."

"I am sorry to hear this news," Nate stated. He was still puzzled about the reason for his friend's visit since the dispute had absolutely nothing to do with him.

"I cherished them both in my heart," Two Owls said solemnly. "When I heard of their deaths, I went off by myself to think. I saw what a waste all this killing has been, and I decided things should be like they were in the old days. The valley should be shared by the two tribes once again." He paused and fixed his inscrutable dark eyes on Nate. "The Utes and the Shoshones must enter into a truce."

"How do you propose going about arranging one?" Nate absently questioned.

The ends of the chief's mouth curled up. "I was hoping you would do that, Grizzly Killer."

"Me?" Nate exclaimed, sitting up. The proposal amazed him, not only because the majority of the Ute nation wouldn't mind roasting him over hot coals, but because his influence in the councils of the Shoshones was extremely limited.

"Hear me out, please, my friend," Two Owls said, raising a hand. He took a sip of his coffee, nodded approval at Winona, and coughed. "I have heard that you are an adopted Shoshone. If so, you have a stake in the welfare of the whole tribe, do you not?"

"It is true I was adopted, but . . ." Nate began.

"But you are not a chief, and your words do not sway many of those who are?" Two Owls had hit the nail on the head.

"Yes."

"You are still a mighty warrior," Two Owls noted. "Even your enemies admit as much. It is widely known that you have defeated the Blackfeet many times. The Bloods and the Piegans fear your medicine. And all have heard about the many brown bears you have killed."

"Even so—" Nate tried again to object, but the chief ignored him.

"If you were to make an appeal to the leaders of the Shoshones, I believe they would listen. Ask them if they would agree to meet with the leaders of my people to discuss a truce. Ask them if they are as tired of the needless bloodshed as I am."

Nate was inclined to refuse. He could see himself going to a lot of trouble for nothing. In the end all he might accomplish would be to drive a wider wedge between those Shoshones who were his friends and those who had vigorously objected to admitting him into the tribe. A small but vocal faction had done their utmost to persuade everyone else that doing so set a bad precedent, that it would bring dire calamity down on the whole nation. Winona had advised him not to take their ranting seriously, that just as there were some whites who hated Indians simply because of the difference in skin color and culture, there were Indians who despised whites for the very same reason. Prejudice knew no racial barriers.

"I have already taken the liberty of contacting the other Ute chiefs," Two Owls was saying. "Messengers were sent asking them to meet me at Bow Valley during the Rose Moon. They have all agreed."

"Did you tell them why you called the council?" Nate asked.

"No. Some would not come if they knew. I would rather surprise them."

"You are taking a great risk. Once they learn the truth, they might turn on you."

"It is a risk I must take," Two Owls signed. "Peace does not come without sacrifice." He swirled his coffee, then took a swallow. "Perhaps this madness can end if we are all willing to put the common good above our own petty feelings."

"Do you realize what you are asking of me?" Nate asked. "I cannot even promise the Shoshones will agree."

"I know you will do your best."

Shaking his head in annoyance, Nate rose and commenced pacing back and forth behind his chair, his hands behind his back. "I'll have to tell them the truth from the start," he said aloud in English. "They'll probably laugh me to scorn, then boot me out of the tribe for making such a harebrained proposal."

"Maybe not," Winona said. "My uncle, Spotted Bull, trusts you. He will go along with whatever you want, and he has the ear of Broken Paw."

"But Broken Paw is only one head chief out of how many? A dozen or so?" Nate pursed his lips, making some fast calculations. The Shoshone nation numbered upwards of six thousand, the majority of which lived in large villages. Pah da-hewak um da was the Shoshone name of their principal chief, although his brother, Moh woom hah, was almost as highly regarded. Under them came the head chiefs of each village, and under these were numerous lesser chiefs. There were also many warriors who enjoyed nearly as much influence as the chiefs and elders, all of whom would have to be convinced that a council with the Utes was in the best interests of the nation before they would consent to it. The more he considered the matter, the more daunting his task seemed.

The core problem, Nate knew, was in the very democratic structure of Indian society, which put the white man's so-called democracy to shame. In the States, whenever politicians took it into their addled heads to put into effect a new law, the people had to go along with the edict whether they liked the law or not. Shoshones were under no such constraints. The head chiefs could suggest policies, but the lesser chiefs and warriors could refuse to go along if they judged the policies to be flawed.

Even in times of war such independent streaks were condoned. A renowned warrior might lead a raid into enemy territory, but those under him were not required to heed his every command, and indeed could do as they saw fit whenever they wanted. Which they often did in order to earn the coup they needed to advance in standing so they could become renowned warriors or even chiefs.

"I reckon my best bet," Nate voiced his thoughts aloud, "is to have a talk with Pah da-hewak um da. If I can persuade him, he can call a general council and maybe persuade the others."

"A fine plan, husband," Winona said. "But it might be prudent to invite Moh woom hah to your meeting also. If you do not, he will feel slighted and refuse to go along with the idea out of hurt pride."

"True," Nate admitted. Sometimes, he reflected, Indian politics was even more complicated than the white variety. He stopped pacing and turned. "Do you have any idea where their villages would be at this time of year?" The question was crucial, since as a general rule villages were seldom kept in one place more than two weeks at a time to prevent sanitary problems.

"Pah da-hewak um da will be at the head of the Snake River. His brother might be on the east branch."

"That's a far piece," Nate remarked. Sitting down again, he addressed their guest. "I will do as you want, Two Owls. Only do not hold it against me if the Shoshones do not come."

The chief reached across the table to affectionately clasp both of Nate's brawny hands. Then he signed, "You have my deepest gratitude, my friend. Between us we might be able to save many lives." Rising, he started for the door. "And now I must go."

"So soon?" Nate asked in surprise. "You are welcome to stay the night. We have plenty of coffee and deer meat, enough for all those who came with you. Why rush off when you have only just arrived?"

"I spread the word among my people that I was going on the warpath against the Arapahos. I must return before some suspect my real reason for leaving."

"I do not understand," Nate said.

"There are some among my tribe who will do all in their power to prevent my people and the Shoshones from meeting," Two Owls revealed.

"You told me they do not know about your wish to hold a council."

The Ute stared at the floor for a moment. "I did tell my wives, and one of them, I fear, may have passed on the information to her relatives. A brother of hers, The Rattler, came to see me a few sleeps before I left. He confided that he knew of my intentions, and he made it plain that he would oppose me if I tried to carry them out."

"Why?"

"The Rattler lost his father to the Shoshones a few winters ago. Now he hates them so much he cannot think about them with a clear head. His heart rules his brain."

"How difficult can he be? What can he do other than tell the other chiefs and try to sway them against you?"

"There is no telling with The Rattler. He is as unpredictable as he is dangerous." A cloud seemed to descend on Two Owls's features. "Let me tell you a story to make my point. Not long ago The Rattler was attracted to a young woman in our village. So was another warrior, Stalking Moon. They courted her as is our custom, and the time came when she made it known that she preferred Stalking Moon. The Rattler was furious. But he was also clever. He began to do little things to anger Stalking Moon, things like inviting Stalking Moon to a feast and having him sit in the least position of honor. There were many such instances, and after each one Stalking Moon was a little angrier. Then came the day that The Rattler let it be known one of his favorite horses was missing. Everyone knew this horse, a white stallion with a black star on its forehead. And soon word spread that it was tied with Stalking Moon's animals."

Nate could see where the tale was leading, and he felt a strong dislike for The Rattler even though he had never met the man.

"The elders gathered," Two Owls had gone on. "Stalking Moon was called before them and asked to explain himself. He said he did not know how the white horse got there. He swore he had not stolen it, and pointed out that doing so would be foolish since the whole village knew who owned it. They accepted his explanation, and he soon returned the horse. The Rattler was smiling when he received the reins. He assured Stalking Moon that he had known all along Stalking Moon would never stoop to thievery. Stalking Moon said nothing, but we all knew how he felt. He wanted revenge for the insults, and he made the mistake one day of questioning The Rattler's courage in the presence of other warriors. The Rattler struck him with his quirt. Enraged, Stalking Moon drew his knife, but was stabbed before he could strike. Everyone agreed that he had been in the wrong by going for his blade, so The Rattler was never punished."

"He sounds dangerous, all right," Nate remarked. "As dangerous as a real rattlesnake."

"So you can see why I must get back to my village quickly," Two Owls said.

Reluctantly, Nate crossed to the door and removed the heavy bar. He propped it against the wall, worked the latch, and motioned for the chief to precede him outside.

"I am sorry I could not stay longer," Two Owls signed

as he advanced. "It would be nice to talk over old times."
He was going to say more, but a streaking shaft suddenly
flashed out of the night and thudded into the front of the
door within inches of his chest.

Chapter Three

Two Owls stood stunned, gaping at the quivering arrow, heedless of being framed in the light of the doorway, a perfect target should the unseen assassin seek to try again.

Intuition impelled Nate to leap, his arms extended. He caught hold of the chief around the waist and bore them both to the hard ground outside as a second deadly shaft cleaved the same space Two Owls had just occupied and thudded into the wood. Nate wound up on top. Rolling to the right, he whipped out a pistol as he rose to his knee. Something moved in the trees to the east, an elusive glimmer of motion hard to pinpoint, and Nate cocked the hammer and snapped off a shot.

At the retort there was a chorus of shouts and cries. From out of the forest south of the cabin poured the warriors in the chief's band, all with their varied weapons at the ready. Mistakenly thinking their leader was being assaulted, some of them charged the one they thought responsible.

Nate saw a tall brave raise a lance to hurl at him. He coiled his legs to jump when a sharp word from Two Owls brought the onrushing warriors up short. Instructions were barked. The Utes immediately fanned out and sped into the woods to the east, going after the real culprit.

"I am in your debt once more, Grizzly Killer," Two Owls signed.

"Who would have done such a thing?" Nate asked, moving to the door in the hope of getting a clue. Since all tribes constructed their arrows a bit differently, identifying the origin of a particular shaft was done by studying how it had been made. Further, warriors invariably painted personal symbols on their arrows so they could identify their shafts should they have to gather some up on a battlefield or elsewhere. There was a practical basis for the practice; arrows took a lot of time and energy to make and were too precious to waste.

But these two, Nate discovered, bore no paint or markings at all. The shafts were plain wood, the fletching added in such a fashion that anyone could have done it. Connecting the arrows to any particular tribe was impossible.

"The one who made these was shrewd like a fox," Two Owls signed angrily.

"It must be one of those who came with you," Nate speculated. "He slipped away from the others, waited for his chance, then rejoined them as they came running up."

"That would be the logical guess."

There was a lot of shouting in the woods as the warriors crisscrossed the terrain seeking some sign of the bowman. Nate was not optimistic. Finding sign at night was always difficult, usually next to impossible, especially if the one being sought did not want to be found. He availed himself of the opportunity to reload, and as he finished the warriors were converging. The same tall one who had nearly speared him spoke at length with Two Owls, who was scowling when he translated for Nate's benefit.

"They found nothing. Whoever it is, I am afraid, will probably try again."

"Will you be safe going back to your people?" Nate asked. "You are welcome to stay here until everything has been set up."

"I am a warrior, not an old woman. My place is in my village." Two Owls rested his hand on Nate's arm briefly, then signed, "Do not let this change your mind. Let nothing stand in your way. Too much is at stake."

"I will do as I promised," Nate vowed. They locked eyes, silently conveying the depth of their commitment.

"May the Great Mystery watch over you," Two Owls signed.

"And you."

The Utes vanished as swiftly as they had initially appeared. Nate caught glimpses of them as they flitted through the pines. He saw one stop and look back. Assuming it was the chief, he smiled and waved, and the figure did the same before fading into the gloom.

"Your friend is a very brave man," Winona said.

Nate nodded and went inside. Both his wife and son had rifles in their hands, which reminded him of the previous incident. "And you're a brave woman," he said tactfully, "but you took an awful risk earlier. If the Utes had been hostile, you'd be dead—or worse."

"I am Shoshone," Winona said simply.

Arguing would have been futile. As any married man could attest, when a woman believed she was in the right, convincing her to change her mind was about as easy as changing the course of a river. So Nate meekly held his tongue and sat down to his long-delayed supper.

Afterward, the family sat in front of the fire and Nate read to them, a daily practice he had started when Zach was still small. Tonight he picked Chapter 22 of *The Last of the Mohicans* by James Fenimore Cooper, one of only five books he owned.

Presently Zach turned in. Nate and Winona cuddled, savoring the tranquility of their home. Then she turned back the blankets on their bed while he tiptoed to the crib he had built a few months after Evelyn was born and lovingly admired her cherubic face.

Before retiring, Nate made certain the flap covering the window was secure. He sat on the edge of the bed to strip off his moccasins and buckskin shirt. Leaving his britches on, he crawled in beside Winona and heard her giggle when his hands found her back.

From the corral rose a strident whinny.

"What now?" Nate groused, sitting up. He was in the mood for loving, not traipsing around in the cold night air.

"Maybe the stallion and the mare are enjoying themselves," Winona suggested impishly.

"That must be it," Nate agreed, eager to lie back down and resume the massage he had begun. No sooner did his shoulder touch the bed than more whinnies caused Evelyn to shift in her sleep and murmur unintelligibly.

"If the baby awakens, I might have to stay up with her until she falls asleep again," Winona mentioned.

"I get your drift," Nate said wearily. Lowering his feet to the floor, he padded to the door and picked up his rifle. "Danged critters," he snapped. "Remind me to shoot one the next time we're low on meat."

"You are not going out like that, are you?" Winona asked.

"I'll be back in two shakes of a lamb's tail," Nate responded, setting the bar down. He wasn't about to waste time dressing and undressing. Stepping into the night, he shivered as gooseflesh broke out all over him. The woods were quiet, as well they should be at so late an hour, but the horses were still acting up, moving about the pen and snorting. They were even more agitated than they had been when they scented the Utes. Suddenly serious, Nate moved slowly forward.

Down in the lake something made a tremendous splash.

A fish? Nate wondered. At the corner he squatted and peered between the pine rails, observing the horses attentively, then focused on the nearby forest. Another bout of shivering made him regret being so impetuous.

The animals came to an abrupt stop, most of them staring eastward.

In the same direction the arrows had come from, Nate mused, rotating on his heels. There was a whizzing sound and a fleeting stinging sensation in his left ear a heartbeat before an arrow smacked into the wall. He threw himself prone, jamming the rifle stock to his shoulder as the hidden bowman loosed a second shaft that nearly parted his hair. Knowing the next one wouldn't miss, Nate rolled to the left. Just in time. An arrow thudded into the earth he had vacated. Frantically he kept on going, rolling over and over and over as rapidly as he could, heading for the open cabin door, keenly aware that if he stopped, he was dead.

Indians were exceptional archers. As well they should be since most boys were taught to use the bow at an early age. By the time they reached manhood they could consistently hit a target the size of a human head from 30 yards away or more. Not only that, a typical bowman could unleash shafts at an incredible rate. Most were able to fire ten to 15 in the time it took a white man to fire a flintlock, reload, and fire again.

So Nate wasn't about to slow down and be transfixed by a half-dozen barbed shafts before he could
regain momentum. He rolled furiously, his hair flying,
his shoulders aching, listening to the impact of several
arrows, one of which clipped his arm, drawing blood.
Then he saw the welcome light cast by the fire's feeble
glow, and at the apex of the next roll he coiled his legs
under him and shot at the entrance.

Yet another arrow struck the doorjamb.

Nate dived through the opening, hit on his left side,
and rolled one final time, away from the exposed portion
of floor.

"Husband!" Winona cried.

Pushing erect, Nate darted to the right side of the doorway, cocked the Hawken, and peeked out. He thought he
heard the crunch of brush receding in the distance, but
he couldn't be positive. Anger almost goaded him into
giving chase, but fortunately common sense prevented
him from being so rash. He slammed the door, then
leaned against the wall and took deep breaths to calm
the wild pumping of his heart and the pounding in his
temples.

Winona was at his side quickly. "How badly are you
hurt?" she asked, gingerly touching the gash on his arm.

"I've got a few scratches, is all," Nate said, raising his
hand to feel his ear. When he brought the hand down, his
fingers were smeared with blood.

"Pa, what is it? What happened?" Zach inquired, hurrying from the corner where his blankets and quilts were
strewn. Over in the crib, Evelyn had awakened and was
waving her tiny arms in the air.

"We have company," Nate said grimly, straightening.
"The same cussed devil that tried to kill Two Owls had
a go at me." Striding to the bed, he swiftly donned his
fringed shirt, moccasins, and beaver hat. His wide belt
went outside his shirt.

"I'll come with you, Pa," Zach offered eagerly.

"You'll stay with your ma and sister," Nate directed. "If something happens to me, they'll need a man to help protect them." He girded his waist with his arsenal and slipped the straps to his powder horn and bullet pouch over his head. Scooping up his rifle from the bed, he made for the door.

Concern mirrored in her dark eyes, Winona blocked his path. "I would be grateful if you would wait until morning."

"He might be long gone by then."

"What if there is more than one? Have you thought of that?"

"Since when do odds bother a mountanee man?" Zach rejoined, adopting a lopsided grin to show her he was funning. She refused, though, to be lighthearted about the prospect of his being killed.

"Let me go with you if you will not take Stalking Coyote," Winona proposed, using the Shoshone name for their son. "I can handle a rifle and pistol well. You have said so yourself."

"That you can," Nate allowed. "But what if Evelyn gets hungry? Zach can't do much for her, can he?" Shaking his head, he gently moved her aside and gripped the latch. "Don't fret on my account. Shakespeare says I'm too ornery to be killed before I'm at least sixty."

"Keep your eyes peeled," Winona said softly.

"Shoot sharp's the word!" Zach added.

Nate let his face reflect his love for them, his gaze lingering on Winona. "Keep the bar in place while I'm gone. And no matter what you hear, don't open up unless I'm right outside telling you to. Savvy?"

Both of them nodded.

"See you shortly," Nate pledged. Quietly lifting the latch, he cracked the door, checked the clear space between the cabin and the trees, then bolted outside

and raced madly for the shelter of the pines. Behind
him the door slammed and there was the thump of the
bar being applied.

A deathly stillness pervaded the forest. In that silence
Nate imagined his breaths were like the puffing of a
steam engine. He dropped to a knee behind a trunk
and scanned the woods. Not so much as a blade of
grass rustled. The wind had died, leaving the forest
as motionless as a graveyard. Was the bowman still
lurking somewhere out there? Nate mused. Or had the
brave left?

Hefting the Hawken, Nate bore northward, relying on
all available cover to screen his movements. His soft
moccasins made no sound on the thick carpet of pine
needles underfoot. Often he stopped to look and listen,
the cardinal rule of surviving in the wild. About 50 yards
from the cabin he bore to the east, taking a game trail
down to the lake shore. There he hunkered down at the
edge of the undergrowth.

The surface of the water resembled polished glass,
so serene was the night. Here and there floated groups
of ducks, geese, and brants, none of which were near
Nate. He focused his attention on the barren strip of
earth, averaging ten feet in width, that encircled the
entire lake. Uppermost in his mind were the sounds
he had heard earlier of someone running eastward. If
that person intended to cover a lot of ground fast, the
easiest route was along the strip bordering the water.

Nate scoured the shoreline once, saw no one, and was
rising to make a search of the woods surrounding his
homestead when faint movement on the southeast shore
sent a tingle of excitement down his spine. Squinting, he
distinguished a lone man trotting toward a point where a
stream flowed out of the lake and down across the valley.

"Got you," Nate said to himself. He raced along the
west side, staying close to the trees so his silhouette

wouldn't be obvious. Pacing his strides, he maintained a brisk clip for over half a mile. By then he was near the east end of the lake and within several hundred yards of the stream.

Nate entered the woods again, but never ventured more than a few feet from the tree line. When he heard low gurgling, he slowed to a walk. On cat's feet he wound among the evergreens until he spied the near bank. Bending at the waist, he crept to a bush and poked his head out to survey the length of the stream. A buzzing sound alerted him to his mistake. He tried to jerk back, but the arrow connected before he could and he felt his hat whipped from his head.

Dashing to a nearby tree, Nate hunched down and mentally cursed himself for being a cocky fool. The warrior must have halted at the mouth of the stream to check if he was being followed and spotted Nate in pursuit. Now the bowman had a fair idea where he was, but had no target to shoot at.

Waiting a full minute, Nate suddenly launched himself at a stand of fir trees. He hadn't gone three steps when a shaft clipped several whangs from the sleeve of his shirt. On the opposite bank a vague shape materialized.

Nate yanked out his right pistol, pointed it at the shape, and hastily fired. The firs closed around him a second later, and since being caught short might prove fatal, he promptly reloaded the spent flintlock. With it in one hand and the rifle in the other, he cautiously flitted from bole to bole, advancing as close to the stream as he safely dared.

So far, Nate realized, Fate had smiled on him. By all rights the warrior should have brought him down. He must be extremely careful from here on; no man's string of luck lasted forever.

The woodland across the way was now deceptively peaceful. Nate raked the shadows for telltale sign of the elusive archer, to no avail. Their conflict had become a battle of wits, a game of cat and mouse, and who was to say which was which? For all Nate knew, at that very moment the warrior might be creeping toward him.

Retreating into the firs, Nate moved eastward. He refused to wait for the enemy to show himself. Going on the offensive was better, in his estimation. So he trekked over a hundred yards downstream, past a bend that would hide his next move, and when he came on a spot where the stream narrowed to a mere few feet, he vaulted the swiftly flowing water and sought the protection of a thicket.

Nate smiled as he thought of how surprised the Indian was going to be. Stepping lightly, he headed for the stretch of forest directly across from the firs. In the back of his mind he mulled the possible motive for the warrior's attack on him at the cabin. Assuming it was the same brave who had attempted to slay Two Owls, what did the man hope to gain? Was it a warrior who objected to making a truce with the Shoshones? Someone who would stop at nothing to disrupt the peace council? Who was going to stop Nate from presenting the idea to them no matter what?

There were a dozen unanswered questions. Nate hoped to learn the truth once he jumped the bowman. His senses quivering in anticipation, he snuck closer and closer to where he believed the man was hiding. So intent was he on locating his quarry, with his eyes riveted straight ahead, that he didn't realize the warrior was much, much nearer until with his peripheral vision he registered the rush of a hurtling form. Pivoting, Nate brought the Hawken up, deflecting the powerful sweep of a knife that would have sliced him open like a melon. He swung the stock at the warrior's head, but the brave was extraordinarily quick and managed to duck under the blow and spring.

Arms banded thick with muscle wrapped around Nate's waist and bore him to the earth. His right knee arced upward, catching the warrior in the groin, flipping the man off. Nate pushed to his feet and tried to bring the rifle to bear, but the Indian wasn't about to let him do any such thing. The knife leaped at his face, forcing Nate backwards, and struck the barrel of the Hawken, jarring his fingers.

Employing the Hawken at close range was impossible. Nate let it fall and snatched at a pistol. The brave swung again, at Nate's midsection, and he had to jerk his hand aside. He settled for the tomahawk instead. The gloom hid most of the brave's features but not the arrogant smirk the man wore. Nate, out of sheer spite, swung his tomahawk at the brave's face and the warrior skipped to the right.

Like awkward dancers the pair now circled one another, each with his weapon held close to his waist, each waiting for the other to make the first move.

Nate noted the wiry frame of his foe, the man's poise and supple grace. He also noted the style of hair: Ute. So his hunch had been right, evidently. His ill-timed reflection was cut short when the warrior unexpectedly leaned forward and started to swing the knife, but Nate, judging it a feint, didn't react, and so was set to dodge when the knife reversed direction and speared at his privates.

Lunging, Nate delivered a blow that would have split the warrior's skull had it landed. Yet once again the Ute was too fast for him and skipped out of harm's reach. Nate tried to press the advantage, swinging repeatedly, missing by a hair with every swipe. The brave made no attempt to block any of the blows, which Nate thought was odd. Then the crack of a twig to his rear showed there was a method to the Ute's madness.

A different pair of arms looped around Nate from behind, pinning his own to his sides. The discovery there were two of them startled Nate so badly that for a few seconds he offered no resistance. Warm breath fanned his neck. Gruff laughter mocked him. He saw the Ute in front elevate the knife for the kill. And instinct took over where reason failed.

"No!" Nate roared, snapping his head backward. The crunch of cartilage verified he had struck the brave's nose, and the hold on him slackened. But the one in front was closing. Nate jammed both heels into the ground, then shoved with all of his might, causing the warrior who was restraining him to stumble rearward. With a savage wrench, Nate tore loose and whirled.

The two Utes were side-by-side, the brave with the crushed nose stooped, blood gushing over his mouth and chin.

Nate had them at his mercy. His left pistol cleared his belt and his thumb curled back the hammer. In another moment he would blast the warrior with the knife into eternity. He was on the verge of prevailing when a feral growl sounded to his right and from out of the night flew a hairy four-legged terror, its jaws clamping down on Nate's wrist so hard the teeth sheared his flesh as if it was butter.

A dog! Nate's mind shrieked as he tried to fling the beast from him. It clung on with terrier perseverance although it was the size of a wolf, its weight dragging his arm down. He clubbed the tomahawk at its head, grazing an ear. In retaliation the animal went into a bestial frenzy, shaking his arm as if trying to rip it from the socket. Grimacing in torment, Nate stepped back to get away from the pair of Utes before they thought to finish him while he was temporarily distracted. His foot bumped a rock and he tripped against a tree.

The Ute armed with the knife was coming toward him.

Nate was in a fix. He couldn't fight off the dog and the brave both. One or the other would be the death of him if he didn't do something, and do it quickly. The pistol was still cocked, still firm in his fingers, even though the dog was doing its best to chew his hand clean off. Gritting his teeth, he held his arm rigid and managed to swing it a few inches to the left so that the barrel was pointed at the onrushing Ute. Aiming was a useless proposition. He simply prayed for the best and squeezed the trigger.

At the retort, the lean Ute clutched at his ribs and doubled over, stopped cold in his tracks.

The dog, however, was roused to a fever pitch of fury by the smoke and the loud blast. It redoubled its assault, worrying Nate's arm as if it was a slab of venison. Nate continued to retreat, bearing the animal with him as he tried to bash in its skull. But in the dark, and with the dog lurching and pitching every which way, he was unable to land a solid blow. His desperation was mounting by the moment when he took another swift step backwards and the ground seemed to vanish from under him. Dismay numbed him as he felt a rush of cool air past his head and he realized he had just plunged over the edge of the bank—into the stream.

Chapter Four

There had been a time when Nathaniel King of New York would have broken out in gooseflesh at the mere thought of being set upon by a vicious dog. But Nate King of the Rocky Mountains had fought panthers and black bears, wolverines and grizzlies. He no longer feared animals. He was wary of them, yes. But when attacked, he became every bit as savage as his bestial adversaries.

This time was no exception. As Nate felt the cold, clammy water of the shallow stream envelop him, he went practically berserk. At this spot the depth was only a foot, enough to soak him thoroughly but not to impede his movements as he surged to his knees and flailed like a madman with his tomahawk at the dog. The animal, unable to get a firm purchase because of the slippery streambed, took two solid blows to the skull, then released its grip and turned to scramble up the bank.

Nate wasn't about to let it escape. He bounded at the beast, the tomahawk glittering dully in the starlight, and sank the keen edge into the dog's side. The animal yelped, twisted away, and scurried to the top, limping as it went over the rim.

As much as Nate wanted to go after the dog and finish it off, he had the Utes to think of. They had bows, and he didn't know how seriously either of them was hurt. He had lost his rifle—which might now be in their hands—and he was losing blood fast from the terrible wound on his left wrist.

Swallowing his anger and his pride, Nate turned and scrambled up the opposite side. Keeping low, he sprinted into the pines and bore to the west, toward the lake. No pursuit had yet materialized, which puzzled him. The Utes should be anxious to run him down and take his hair.

A spruce tree bearing branches low to the ground afforded Nate the hiding place he needed. Squatting, he worked his way to the trunk and sat with his back to it. The wind was picking up, swaying the tops of the trees and shaking the brush, denying him the aid of his ears in detecting the warriors.

Sliding the tomahawk under his belt, Nate drew his other pistol and set both down in front of him. The water had rendered the loaded flintlock useless, so he had to reload both. Uncapping the powder horn, he set about doing so. His right arm was lanced by shooting spasms every time he moved, but he steeled his mind against the agony and forced his fingers to work as they should.

Since Nate lacked the means to dry the guns completely, he couldn't be certain they would discharge when he needed them. It was a chance he would have to take because he wasn't going back without his prized Hawken. To a free trapper struggling to survive in the wilderness a rifle meant the difference between life and death. And although Nate owned spare rifles, he was so fond of the Hawken that he had given it a name: Hawkeye, after the hero of James Fenimore Cooper's novels.

Nate's arm was throbbing abominably when he finished and secured the pistol at his waist. Gingerly tugging the sleeve up to his elbow, he examined the wound. The dog's teeth had shorn through almost to the bone on the top but not so deep on the bottom. Blood still seeped out, although there was less and less each minute.

Nothing could be done until Nate got back to the cabin. Pressing the wrist to his side, he filled his left hand with a flintlock and crawled into the open. Every sense primed, he slanted through the trees to the stream and down into the water. To recover his Hawken he must move swiftly, before the loss of blood took its toll or his arm became so painful he couldn't use it at all.

It was an eerie feeling, silently moving through the murk of the forest knowing there were two murderous braves and a ferocious dog out there somewhere looking to have their revenge on him. Nate made slow time since he had to stop every few feet to scan the woods.

Presently Nate was in the general vicinity of where he had tangled with the Utes. Since they had still not shown themselves, he speculated they might have lit out, a logical assumption particularly if the one he had shot was bad off. He began working in a zigzag pattern to cover more area, scouring the grass and rocks.

At length Nate halted, studying the closest trees. He was fairly sure the fight had taken place right at that spot, so he spent the next half an hour going over every square inch, stooped at the waist to see better. With each passing minute his discouragement grew, and he had about resigned himself to having to return during the light of day when he noticed a long dark streak in a patch of weeds. Eagerly he clutched at it and triumphantly lifted his Hawken on high.

By now Nate's arm was causing him terrible misery. From his shoulder to his fingers it seemed to be pulsing in rhythm with the beating of his heart. Gritting his teeth against the anguish, Nate bent his steps homeward. Bouts of weakness assailed him, each more potent than the one before.

Reaching the lake took three times as long as it should. Nate knelt by the water's edge and slowly dipped his arm in, smiling in satisfaction when the pain reduced somewhat. The frigid water only had a temporary effect, unfortunately, so he was soon hurrying westward along the south shore.

Perhaps a mile had been covered when Nate experienced a fleeting ripple of dizziness. Holding his head high, he forged on, covering another 25 yards. Then more severe dizziness elicited a groan and caused him to stagger as if drunk. "Damn," he muttered in frustration. The prospect of passing out was distinctly unappealing. Should a wandering grizzly or other predator stumble on him, he'd never open his eyes again.

Abruptly, the dizziness subsided. Nate availed himself of the reprieve and trotted toward the trail leading up to the cabin, resisting every step of the way the tidal wave of agony that was doing its utmost to swamp him. He was nearly there when a creature materialized out of the trees, a four-legged creature slinking low to the ground.

"The dog!" Nate blurted out, and tried to raise the Hawken to shoot. His right arm was sluggish to respond, his hand almost numb. The beast came closer and closer, the white spot on its chest standing out like the white stripe of a polecat. Nate pulled a pistol with his left hand, curled his thumb around the hammer, and took a bead.

"Now you're gone beaver, you mangy varmint!" Nate declared, steadying his aim. He was in the act of cocking the gun when two words screamed in his brain: *White spot?* He glanced at the mark again, blinked, and laughed lightly. "Well, I'll be doggone!"

Blaze came up to him and sniffed, apparently disturbed by the fresh scent of blood.

"Fancy meeting you," Nate said weakly. "Where were you a while ago when I could have used some help? Off prancing with some she-wolf, I reckon." He bent over to give the wolf a pat. Like a lance spearing through his skull, the dizziness flared again, and this time it brought him to his knees. He clenched his eyes shut and doubled over, hoping the attack would end soon so he could get to his destination.

Something moist brushed his cheek.

Nate looked up and received another lick on the forehead. "You stupid critter," he muttered. "I can't pet you when I'm halfway to being crow bait." He tried to push the wolf away, but the movement aggravated his dizziness. "If you want to be useful, go fetch Zach and Winona. Hear me? Go fetch them."

Blaze cocked his head and whined.

"Go, blast you!" Nate urged sternly. "Fetch Zach!"

While accustomed to living with humans, the wolf was far from domesticated, and had proven extremely difficult to train even to go outside to relieve itself. On many occasions Zach and Nate had tried to teach Blaze how to go after tossed sticks, with limited success. So Nate wasn't at all surprised that the wolf turned at his command and raced into the woods heading due south instead of due west.

"Idiot," Nate muttered. The dizziness was gone, enabling him to stand and hurry to the trail. Inky shadows closed over him once he was among the trees.

Every stride took considerable effort, and once, when
he inadvertently bumped his right arm with the Hawken,
compounding his torture, he barely checked a shriek.

"Oh, Lord," Nate breathed, licking his dry lips. He
longed for a glimpse of the cabin. The next bend produced just that, and elated he shuffled ahead. Then,
behind him, he heard the patter of someone or something
rushing to overtake him. Pausing, he glanced around and
grinned at the sight of Blaze bearing down like a bat
out of hell. "What the devil?" he wondered aloud, and
was even more surprised when he saw that Blaze was
favoring the legs on one side.

Too late Nate realized there was no white mark on
the animal's chest. He extended the pistol he held, yet
he might as well have been moving in slow motion for
all the good it did him. The dog snarled and leaped,
barreling into his chest, its front legs striking his right
arm.

Nate cried out as he went down. He swung the rifle
in front of his face and neck, protecting them from the
dog's snapping fangs. Claws ripped into his buckskin
shirt. Saliva dripped onto his face. His shoulder rip-
pling, he tried swatting the dog off, but he lacked the
strength. He needed to use both arms; the right was
virtually useless. The fangs drew inch by inch nearer
to his vulnerable throat as the dog pressed its assault.

Death hung over Nate King in the shape of the fiend-
ish canine's distorted features when another element was
added to their somber life-and-death conflict. From out
of nowhere hurtled a second hairy form, only this one
plowed into the dog instead of Nate. In the blink of an
eye the forest was filled with horrendous gnashing and
gnarling and the crash of wildly tumbling bodies through
the brush.

Nate rose on the elbow of his good arm and watched
helplessly as the fierce clash raged. He dared not try to

shoot the dog in his condition; he might hit Blaze by mistake.

The wolf and the Ute mongrel were about equal in size. Their speed was also roughly the same. In inherent ferocity neither could claim superiority. And there was a chance, since it was not uncommon for village dogs to stray into the wild and mate with their wild brethren, that the dog had wolf blood pumping in its veins. But the dog was wounded, and in the end that was the deciding factor.

Sitting up, Nate saw the pair smash into a bush. The collision knocked them apart and both immediately scrabbled upright. The dog was the slower of the two. As it rose, one of its legs slipped, and before it could regain its footing the wolf was upon it, razor teeth sinking into its throat. Yelping, the dog tried to pull loose. Blaze hung on, jerking his head from side to side, doing to the dog what the dog had previously done to Nate's wrist. Seconds later the clash was all but over although Blaze continued to worry the mongrel's neck.

"Husband!"

The sharp cry brought Nate to his feet. He turned to find his wife and son speeding toward him, Winona bundled in a heavy buffalo robe, Zach wearing only his leggings, each armed with a rifle. "Just in time," he told them as they slowed. "I'm about plumb tuckered out."

"What happened?" Winona asked anxiously, glancing at the two animals. "Is that another wolf?" She looked at him, at his arm, and suddenly she was on her knees inspecting his wrist. "You're hurt! Hurt bad!"

"My arm does sting a little," Nate said, trying to make light of the situation. "I could use some of that herbal tincture of yours."

"We must get you inside," Winona said, taking his hand in hers and pulling him along. "Zach, run ahead and start water boiling for tea."

"Yes, Ma." The boy was off like the proverbial shot.

"He's a darn good son," Nate said proudly. "Knows how to listen to his folks without giving them aggravation all the time like those pampered kids back in the States." He forced a grin. "You could take some lessons from him."

"What do you mean?"

"I thought I told you to keep the bar in place until you heard my voice."

"Since when does a wife listen to every word her husband says?"

"Hardly ever," Nate grumbled. "But I'd be a happy man if you'd listen just *once*."

In the glare of the burning logs Zach had tossed onto the fire, the wound was sickening to look at. The flesh had been mangled, some of the skin hung in strips. Veins and arteries had been uncovered and one had been severed.

"Gosh, Pa," the boy said. "If that was me, I'd be crying my lungs out. Doesn't the pain get to you?"

"I hardly noticed it."

Winona made Nate sit on the bed. She helped strip off his shirt, then took a beaded parfleche off a peg on the wall and spread out the contents beside him. There were dried plants, roots, pouches of herbs, and other Shoshone remedies for ailments as diverse as sprains and smallpox. Some of them Nate recognized, such as *sammabe,* as the Shoshones called juniper leaves, which were used to make a tea that was helpful in the treatment of rheumatism. There was *pannonzia,* or yarrow, used for toothaches and a variety of other conditions. And there was honeysuckle root, which the Shoshones relied on to treat swellings.

"Did you find the one who tried to kill Two Owls and you?" Winona asked as her preparations unfolded.

Nate detailed his encounter, keeping the account short and sweet, and said nothing to indicate how close he had come to meeting his Maker.

Not fooled in the least, Winona commented when he was done, "Your guardian was watching over you this night. If you are not careful, one day you will go too far and I will have to cut off another finger."

The reminder drew Nate's gaze to her hand. Years ago, on losing her father and mother to the Blackfeet, she had chopped two of her fingers off at the first joint as a token of her grief. The practice was one of the few Shoshone customs that he found personally revolting, but no amount of persuasion on his part had sufficed to change her mind. When a loved one died, grief must be displayed. That was the way it had always been; that was the way it would always be.

For the next hour Winona hovered over him, ministering her poultices and ointments. She cut strips off an old blanket, washed them in a bucket, and applied them as bandages. As she tucked the end of the last strip under, she smiled down at him and commented, "We will not be able to leave for six or seven sleeps now, but Two Owls will understand the delay."

"We leave the day after tomorrow," Nate informed her.

"That is too soon. Your wrist needs more time to heal. If it was my decision, we would not go for a full moon."

"The day after tomorrow."

"You are being stubborn. What difference would a few more sleeps make?"

"Two Owls is counting on me to have the Shoshones arrive at Bow Valley in time. Time is tight. Any delay is costly."

"What if your wrist becomes infected?"

Grinning, Nate stroked her chin. "I'm not fretting. The best healer in the world is taking care of me."

"Your flattery is wasted," Winona said indignantly, rising in a huff. "And you have your nerve to talk about *wives!*"

Nate reverted to the Shoshone tongue and said softly, "I love you." But she ignored him and walked over to sit down in the rocking chair. Closing his eyes, he gave thought to soothing her ruffled feathers. Lethargy set in before he could, the warmth and the security combining to send him to sleep despite his best intentions.

The feeling of a warm body cuddled next to his brought Nate fully awake. He twisted his head and found Winona sound asleep, her features incredibly lovely in the rosy light from the crackling fire. A heavy blanket covered both of them. Smiling, he kissed her soft cheek, then glanced at Zach, who lay asleep in the corner, snoring softly.

A feeling of supreme satisfaction flooded Nate's inner being with profound happiness. There were times, such as now, when he rated himself the most fortunate man alive. He had been blessed with a marvelous family, he was living where he preferred to live, in the often violent but always gloriously stirring Rockies, and he had a sturdy roof over his head. What more could a man ask for?

Well, there was one thing, Nate reflected. He was thankful for the freedom he enjoyed, a freedom such as he had never known back in the States, the true freedom to do as he wanted at any time of the day or night without answering to any man. Of course, with that freedom came tremendous responsibility. Every action, every word, had to be weighed carefully, because a single mistake might cost him his life and a single tactless word might result in bloodshed.

Civilization coddled the people living under its influence. It gave a false sense of security by protecting them from their own folly. If a man insulted another, the offending party might lash out with insults in return, or perhaps even beat the stuffing out of the offending party, but the one insulted would never think to do anything more drastic because the stern arm of the law would punish him if he did. So men were at liberty to treat one another as shabbily as they desired without fear of grave consequences.

All that was much different in the wild where an unwritten natural law held sway. Should a man be so foolish as to insolently heap an indignity on someone else, the offender might well wind up dead. Insults were never, ever tolerated by whites or Indians. Every man had responsibility for everything he said or did, and he knew if he took that responsibility lightly he might soon be worm food.

There were some who claimed such behavior was barbaric. Nate didn't agree. In his estimation the civilized viewpoint was the incorrect one since it allowed those with savage or spiteful streaks or those who were just plain wicked to prey on those who were peace-loving without fear of retribution.

Handling responsibility well was the earmark of maturity. What did that say about the many civilized folks who were unwilling to accept that fact and live accordingly? Sometimes Nate wondered if all those laws the politicians were so fond of imposing were no more than substitutes for personal responsibility intended to make sure the immature didn't get completely out of hand.

Nate gazed fondly at his son, musing on whether the boy had any idea how lucky he was to be reared among the regal peaks and valleys of the mountains and not among the constricting streets and alleys of some city or town. Did the boy even recognize the importance of being able to roam at will and not having to mold his growing manhood the way others would have him do?

Probably not, Nate decided. Youngsters that age pretty much took things for granted. Somehow, Nate must instill in Zach the same love for freedom that Nate had.

Suddenly there was a light scratching sound at the door.

Lifting his head, Nate listened. When the scratching was repeated, he eased out of bed without waking his wife, and briskly crossed the floor. Not until then did he realize his wrist no longer throbbed. Winona's herbal treatment was doing wonders for the wound.

A familiar whine greeted Nate at the door. He lifted the bar with his right hand, then worked the latch quietly and stood back so Blaze could enter. "You've sure got me trained," he whispered. The wolf whined and sniffed at his legs as he replaced the bar.

On the bed Winona moved, rolling onto her back, and mumbled in Shoshone, but she didn't awaken.

"Here," Nate said, moving to the counter where several strips of venison had been laid out so they would be handy when Winona fixed breakfast. He took the largest, squatted, and dangled the tantalizing morsel over the animal's head. "This is for saving my hide."

In a single gulp Blaze snatched and swallowed the meat.

"You might enjoy your food more if you didn't wolf it down all the time," Nate commented. Then, realizing what he had said, he burst into laughter and had to cover his mouth with his hand so as not to disturb his loved ones.

Blaze eyed him expectantly.

"I know my life is worth more than a single measly piece," Nate said, "and tomorrow I'll see that you get a thick chunk for your trouble. How's that?" Giving the wolf a pat, he stood and returned to bed.

Once under the blanket, Nate wrapped his good arm around his wife and pressed flush against her. Her warm breath fluttered against his neck, tickling him, and coming as it did on top of his inadvertent comment to Blaze, it triggered a new round of merriment. The bed began to shake as he buried his face in the pillow and laughed until he couldn't laugh anymore. It had been ages since he last enjoyed such hearty mirth, and he figured it was due in part to his harrowing experience across the lake, sort of a release for all his pent-up tension. Still chuckling, he looked at Winona, and was dismayed to find her wide-eyed and studying him as if he was demented.

"Are you done trying to break the bed, husband?"

"Sorry," Nate blurted out. "I don't know what got into me. I didn't mean to wake you."

"You should be sleeping," Winona chided, reaching up to check his brow. "Your skin is still very warm. If you keep acting foolish, it will take you much longer to heal. I want you to make yourself comfortable and lie still."

"Yes, dear," Nate said. He had to suppress a snicker at his next thought: What was that he had been pondering about freedom? For a married man there was no such thing!

Chapter Five

"Pa, I think we're being followed."

Nate reined up and swung his black stallion so he could scan their back trail. They were eight days along on their journey, strung out in single file with him in the lead, Winona next on a mare leading one pack animal, and Zach bringing up the rear with the other. He scoured the valley they had just traversed, but saw no hint of movement. "What did you see, son?"

"Two riders, moving quick," Zach answered, pointing at the slope of a mountain to the' west. "I just had a glimpse of them before they went into some trees. But they were Indians, Pa, sure enough."

Winona stopped next to Nate. "The two you tangled with before we left. You were right. They did trail us, just as you expected."

Nate nodded. "Based on their actions so far, I'd say they'll stop at nothing to prevent us from reaching the Shoshones." He indicated the country ahead. "Between

here and the Snake River region they'll make their
move."

"What do we do, Pa?" Zach asked.

"We keep on going," Nate replied. "So far they have
no idea we know they're shadowing us, which gives us
an edge."

"We could bushwhack them."

"If the opportunity comes along, I'll try," Nate said.
"But it won't be easy. They'll be on guard every step of
the way." He resumed riding northwestward, his right arm
resting on his thigh. The wound was mending nicely, as
wounds invariably did in the clean, rarified mountain air,
but as yet he could not use his right hand for more than a
minute or so without causing pain to flare up.

The past eight days had been largely uneventful. Abundant wildlife was everywhere in evidence; deer, elk,
bighorn sheep, and mountain buffalo were encountered
almost daily. Twice they had seen grizzlies, and each
time the huge bears had promptly reversed direction and
disappeared in the woods, much to Nate's relief. Grizzlies
were notoriously fickle; the same bear might run from
humans one day and charge the next.

Nate had been especially alert for Indian sign. They
had come on an old trail made several days ago by a
large hunting or war party. Other than that, they had
seen nothing to cause alarm until Zach spied the pair
on the mountain. Now they must be extra vigilant.

On several occasions Nate had been through the stretch
of rugged country they were in, so he knew it fairly well.
While not the normal route he took when going to visit
Winona's kin, it would shave two days off their time if
a certain high pass was clear of snow.

For the rest of the afternoon Nate repeatedly sought
the two Utes. They never showed themselves again,
though, leaving him to conjecture on where they were
and what their strategy might be. He tried putting himself

Join the Western Book Club and GET 4 FREE* BOOKS NOW!
A $19.96 VALUE!

Yes! I want to subscribe to the Western Book Club.

Please send me my **4 FREE* BOOKS**. I have enclosed $2.00 for shipping/handling. Each month I'll receive the four newest Leisure Western selections to preview for 10 days. If I decide to keep them, I will pay the Special Members Only discounted price of just $3.36 each, a total of $13.44, plus $2.00 shipping/handling ($19.50 US in Canada). This is a **SAVINGS OF AT LEAST $6.00** off the bookstore price. There is no minimum number of books I must buy, and I may cancel the program at any time. In any case, the **4 FREE* BOOKS** are mine to keep.

> *In Canada, add $5.00 shipping/handling per order for the first shipment. For all future shipments to Canada, the cost of membership is $16.25 US, which includes shipping and handling. (All payments must be made in US dollars.)

NAME: _____

ADDRESS: _____

CITY: _____ **STATE:** _____

COUNTRY: _____ **ZIP:** _____

TELEPHONE: _____

E-MAIL: _____

SIGNATURE: _____

in their place, and didn't like the conclusion he reached, namely that they might strike much sooner than he had thought, perhaps even in the next three or four days to make certain Winona, Zach, and he didn't get anywhere near Shoshone territory. After the fourth day, even though they would still have a considerable distance to cover before they came on any Shoshone villages, they would be in a region the Shoshones routinely hunted in, and might stumble on a band that would escort them the rest of the way. The Utes couldn't let that happen.

That evening, as Nate sat by the fire munching pemmican, he commented, "I figure it's wise to have one of us on watch at all times from here on out, so we'll divide the night up three ways. Zach, you'll go first. Winona can sit up after you're done. And I'll go last." He didn't bother to mention that the last stint would be the most dangerous since Indians traditionally liked to attack their enemies right before dawn, no doubt because that was when most people were in the soundest sleep and sentries were starting to doze off themselves.

"You can count on me, Pa," Zach said excitedly. "No darn Ute is going to lift our hair if I have anything to say about it."

Before retiring Nate checked the horses, insuring they were firmly tied. He arranged the saddles, packs, and parfleches in a ring a few yards out from the fire for some added protection. Then, the Hawken at his side and both pistols loose under his belt, Nate reclined on his back, his hands under his head. Across from him Winona was doing the same, while Zach sat down on one of the packs, his back to the forest.

"Son?" Nate said softly.

"Don't worry. I'll wake Ma on time."

"It's not that." Nate nodded at the fire. "Eyes take a while to adjust between light and darkness. What if you hear something while you're sitting there staring into the fire? You wouldn't be able to see a thing when you turn around."

"Oh. Sorry."

"Don't be. No one knows all there is to know the moment they're born. One of the purposes of living is to learn as we go along."

"Sometimes it seems like it will take forever for me to cram all the stuff I need into my brain."

"A parson would say it's supposed to take that long."

"It sure is hard sometimes. I mean, how do you manage to remember all the little things?"

"Practice, son. If you do something long enough it starts to come easy."

Winona giggled. "And having a wife to remind you whenever you forget also helps."

"Which wives do, every chance they get," Nate confirmed.

Quiet descended on the camp except for the crunching of the horses as they grazed on the sweet grass, the snap-crackle-pop of the fire, and the sigh of the wind through the trees.

Nate doubted he would be able to sleep, not with the threat of the Utes hanging over their heads. But he reckoned without the effect of their hard day of travel and the high altitude. Before he knew it, he was out to the world.

Young Zach heard his father utter a series of snorts, and looking over his shoulder saw that Nate was asleep. His mother also appeared to have drifted off. The knowledge that their lives were in his hands made him grip his rifle more firmly. He must be vigilant until his mother relieved him.

The dancing firelight caused bizarre shadows to dance around the perimeter of their camp. Zach, as boys often do, lent life to the shifting shapes where none existed.

He imagined one to be a stalking bear, another a slinking panther, his nervousness mounting to where he just had to jump up and make a circuit of the camp.

The horses were peacefully bedding down. Zach counted on them to let him know if something came near. Their superior hearing and sense of smell enabled them to detect predators or hostiles far off, so he kept an eye on them at all times.

For two hours all went well. Then, with Zach resting on his saddle, wearily fighting off waves of fatigue, the black stallion nickered. Instantly Zach was awake and on his feet. Remembering what his father had once said about exposing himself, he jumped behind the saddle and crouched.

Off in the trees something was moving. Brush crackled as if from the passage of a large form. A tree limb broke with a loud crack.

Zach gulped and jammed his rifle to his shoulder. Was it a horse? he wondered. Or a bear? Whatever, it was coming closer and closer. Soon it would be right outside the camp.

A shriek for his parents was on Zach's lips when he spied a dark four-legged shape moving rapidly through the forest on a bearing that would take the animal past the camp, not into it. He started to cock his rifle anyway, in case it should swerve toward him. The next second he distinguished the general outline of the creature and identified it as a harmless elk, a bull from the size of the thing.

Relaxing, Zach frowned, upset by his display of fear, and lowered his rifle. He must keep a tighter rein on his imagination, he told himself, or he would never grow up to be a noted warrior like his father. And above all else, that was his goal in life. The name of Grizzly Killer was known far and wide, highly regarded by many and feared by some. It was rumored that even the dreaded Blackfeet, the most powerful tribe west of the Mississippi, regarded Grizzly Killer as a worthy enemy, and every warrior in the nation was eager to be the one to add Grizzly Killer's hair to his collection of scalps.

Turning, Zach watched his folks as they slept. He was thankful for having two such wonderful parents to help guide him through life, and he longed to show them his gratitude for the love and care they had bestowed on him by one day becoming a man they would be proud of. There would come a time, he promised himself, when the name of Stalking Coyote would be as widely respected as that of Grizzly Killer, when he would be a credit not only to his folks but to the Shoshone tribe as well. They would talk of the many coups he counted for years to come.

Another twig snapped in the woods, prompting Zach to idly pivot on his heel. He saw the horses were all upright, gazing nervously after the departing elk. To calm them and keep them from waking his parents, he headed over, and he was almost there when he realized that he was wrong. The horses weren't, in fact, staring at the elk; they were looking at something much nearer, at the edge of the pines.

Puzzled, Zach halted and tried to see what they were seeing. There were trees and bushes and clumps of weeds, but nothing out of the ordinary. Maybe they imagined that they saw something, he reflected, just as he had earlier. Chuckling at their stupidity, he advanced a few more yards.

Movement registered in the corner of Zach's eye. Stopping again, he swung toward the wall of murky vegetation, seeking the source. But he saw the same scene as before. Not so much as a leaf or pine needle had changed position.

Further mystified, Zach took a step, then, racked by uncertainty and not wanting to be caught unawares should there actually be a menace prowling nearby, angled toward the woods. There was a boulder in his path, which he had started to swing around when one of the horses whinnied. Zach glanced back, put a finger to his lips, and said softly, "Shhhhhhhh! you dunderhead."

Facing forward, Zach abruptly drew up in mid-stride. The boulder had moved while his attention was distracted, had uncoiled and risen from the ground, assuming the proportions of a muscular brave who even as Zach set eyes on him leaped at Zach and seized hold of the rifle.

Instinctively Zach held fast. He tried to shout for help, to alert his parents, but his vocal chords refused to cooperate. It was as if they were frozen solid. The warrior's fist leaped at his face and he narrowly evaded the blow. Hauling rearward, he tried to tear his rifle loose, but the warrior was far stronger. He felt the gun slipping from his grasp, and it was fear of losing his rifle more than anything else that spurred him to tilt back his head and bellow, "Pa! Ma!"

Winona came out of a sound sleep with all her senses fully primed, a feat Shoshone girls learned to do at a very early age if they hoped to avoid capture during one of the many raids made by enemy tribes. She was rising, her rifle in her hands, before the sound of her son's shout had died away. With one look she comprehended the danger and dashed to Stalking Coyote's aid.

Someone else was a shade faster. Winona saw her husband charge, saw the pistol in Nate's hand. But the Ute saw it too, and he suddenly gave Zach a shove that sent the boy crashing into Nate. Both went down. Nimbly as a bobcat, the Ute whirled and dashed into the forest, covering the ground in prodigious bounds.

Winona took swift aim. She had the hammer back, her finger on the trigger, when the warrior made a sharp turn and vanished in the shelter of some pines. Upset at his escape, she vented her husband's favorite oath: "Damn!"

Nate had disentangled himself from Zach and stood glaring into the darkness. "I should go after him," he said.

"With one of your arms almost no use at all?" Winona responded. Although she never admitted as much to him, she often worried that his impetuous nature would one day be the cause of his death. "And remember," she prudently added. "There are two of them. You would be outnumbered."

"I know, but I hate to let him get away knowing full well he'll try again the first chance he gets," Nate said.

Zach was straightening, his features crestfallen. "I'm sorry," he said contritely. "He surprised me. I didn't see him until it was too late."

Winona stepped to his side and put a hand on his head. "Are you hurt?" she asked in Shoshone.

"Just my pride."

"You did well. None of us were harmed."

"I should have done better. A true warrior wouldn't have let himself be tricked like I was."

"All warriors are boys first, and boys learn from their mistakes," Winona reminded him. She stepped over to her husband, who was intently studying the woodland. "Do you think he is gone?"

"For now." Nate let down the hammer on his pistol and slid the flintlock under his belt. "We're lucky it was just the one and not both or they might have slit Zach's throat before we could be of any help." He paused, his brow furrowed. "One of them, most likely the warrior I shot, must be bad hurt."

Zach joined them. "But why didn't the one who jumped me just kill me right off? He could have put an arrow into me with no trouble at all."

"I don't rightly know," Nate said, "unless they have some crazy notion of taking Winona and you captive so they can show you off to the other Utes when they get back."

"All he seemed interested in was my rifle," Zach commented.

"There is the explanation," Winona said. "He was hiding nearby spying on us, and when he saw you on guard all alone he figured he could take your gun right out of your hands."

"That makes sense, Ma," Zach said. "The coup would count more that way."

"Yes, it would," Winona confirmed, pleased he understood. The counting of coup was widespread among practically all the Western tribes. It was a means of gauging manhood, of determining who was qualified to bear the title of warrior. In effect, men attained higher standing by earning more and more coups. Among the Shoshones, the Crows, and others, any man who had *not* counted coup by his twentieth winter was made to work with the women and denied the right to sit at council. Small wonder, then, that the braves competed so fiercely to outdo themselves in warfare.

Coup honors were graded according to the deed. Among all Indians, a higher coup was accorded to those who struck enemies with their bare hands or with a coup stick or lance. It took little bravery to slay a foe from afar with a bow or rifle, but great courage to rush up to an armed adversary and engage him at close quarters.

Some tribes allowed a coup to be earned for the stealing of horses and guns. The latter, especially, were highly prized since they were so hard to obtain. So Winona could readily see why the Ute had tried to wrest the rifle from her son by brute force rather than kill the boy and take it, and she gave thanks to the Great Mystery that the warrior had let his craving for recognition get the better of his judgment.

Nate, evidently certain the threat had passed, scrutinized Zach from head to toe. "Are you up to standing watch a while longer? If you're rattled one of us can take over for you."

"I'm Stalking Coyote," the boy said indignantly. "I do not get rattled just because a mangy Ute shows his face. You and Ma can go back to sleep, and I'll wake her like we agreed when it's time."

"As you wish," Nate said.

Winona suppressed a grin when he winked at her. Arms linked, they strolled back to the fire and sat down on their respective blankets. "I am so proud of him," she confided.

"Me too," Nate said, "but I'm keeping one eye open until it's your turn. I wouldn't put it past that darn Ute to slink on back here."

"Then there will be two eyes on him," Winona confided. She leaned down to check on Evelyn, who was snug in her cradleboard and fast asleep. "I am amazed sometimes at the noise our daughter sleeps through."

"Maybe she's hard of hearing," Nate said. "We should test her and find out. Remind me tomorrow and I'll fire off a pistol next to her ear to see how she reacts."

"You do, and I will fire one into your foot to see how you react."

"I'm just trying to help."

"I know, dearest," Winona said sweetly, lying down with her arm draped over their daughter. "But would it not work just as well if we whispered in her ears? If she hears us, she will show it."

"I suppose," Nate said. "But it would be a lot easier to tell with a gunshot."

"Did you hear that, Blue Flower?" she asked the child. "You should be very grateful you have me for a mother."

*   *   *

Nate snorted as he made himself comfortable on his back. He put one arm under his head and the other across his forehead, just above his eyes, which spared them from the glare of the firelight and at the same time permitted him to peek out at Zach without being detected.

The incident had left Nate greatly disturbed. Proud as he was of his son, he was scared to his core of losing the boy. Many times had he reflected that the possibility of losing a child was one of the worst fears a parent entertained, even more so than the death of a mate. The reason was simple. Children were undeniably precious. All parents expected to pass on sooner or later and had learned to live with the likelihood, but when the same parents regarded their own children, who were so young and innocent and bubbling with vitality, they quite naturally wanted their offspring to live on indefinitely.

Adding to Nate's agitation was the Ute's attempt to steal the gun. He thought Winona's idea about the warrior trying to earn greater coup was valid, but at the same time he was amazed the Ute had taken such a blatant risk and in the process alerted them to his presence. He couldn't shake the nagging feeling there must be more to it, that the Ute had an ulterior motive for what he had done. But what could it be?

Like a bolt of lightning illuminating the heavens, insight flared in Nate's mind and he jerked up, his gaze roving over the saddles, the packs, and the horses. The first thing he noticed was that one of the parfleches had disappeared, a bag containing part of their supply of food. The second thing was more critical; one of the horses was missing.

"Wagh!" Nate exploded, showing his rage Indian fashion. While there were no Indian curse words— leading some misguided souls back in the States to mistakenly believe that Indians were more noble than whites—the Indian had a colorful and effective manner of expressing anger or displeasure. As in all else Indians did, they imitated the animal world. Warriors, when aroused, gave vent to the same sort of sound a riled grizzly made, a rumbling grunt-snarl that adequately expressed their feelings just as Nate's cry now expressed his at finding he had been duped.

Leaping up, Nate ran to where the animals were tethered. He wanted to smack himself in the head with his own tomahawk for not noticing sooner, for not seeing that the attempt to steal the gun had been a diversion so the other brave could sneak into the camp unnoticed. The missing horse was one of the pack animals, a reliable pinto he had obtained from the Flatheads a while back. Which figured. Indians were more partial to pintos than any other kind of horse, except for the Nez Percé, who were fond of their special Palouse breed.

Winona and Zach had raced over.

"It's all my fault," the boy said sadly.

"Nonsense," Nate said. "No one is to blame. They skunked us, plain and simple. Be glad they didn't take them all." He gave the black stallion a pat. "Maybe the warrior tried, and Midnight here came close to bashing his head in."

"Is anything else missing?" Winona asked, looking at their possessions.

"The parfleche with our jerky in it," Nate revealed.

"Why the dickens would they take that?" Zach questioned.

"Either they haven't had time to do much hunting on their own," Nate speculated without conviction, "or they just want to make it harder on us to get where we're going."

"But stealing the jerky won't bother us much. We can

live off the land as we go along," Zach said. "They must know that."

"You'd think so," Nate allowed. He went to each of the horses and verified none of the other tethers had been tampered with. Unlike many of his fellow trappers, who secured their animals at night to a single rope, Nate took the time to pound wooden stakes into the ground and tie each horse separately. A single rope, in his estimation, made it ridiculously easy for anyone to come along and steal stock with a single slice of a knife. By using the tactic he did, he made it more difficult for would-be horse thieves by forcing them to cut through a rope for each and every animal, which took longer and increased the odds of being found out.

"This is all becoming very strange," Winona commented. "These Utes are not acting like Utes should."

"What could they be up to?" Zach asked.

"Who can say?" Nate replied. "But something tells me we'll find out sooner or later, and we won't like it one bit when we do."

Chapter Six

The village of Chief Broken Paw was situated in a picturesque valley between the diverging forks of a bubbling stream. There were 356 lodges in all, arranged in traditional order, covering acres and acres of ground. Among them played carefree children, many of the girls using dolls crafted by their mothers or grandmothers, while the boys ran around with small bows or lances imitating the valiant deeds they would one day perform as grown men. Dogs were plentiful, and they were owned not merely as pets, but as beasts of burden when the village was on the move and as sentries at other times. They served an added purpose when the hunting of game produced meager results; they were plunked into pots of boiling water and afterward eaten with relish, dog meat being considered a delightful delicacy.

Most numerous of all in the village were women since they outnumbered the men by a two-to-one margin. There were scores upon scores of them, busily curing hides or mending or making clothes or cooking or engaged in a variety of other tasks. And unlike some of their white sisters, who viewed all work related to the home as menial and beneath their dignity, the Shoshone women took great pride in being able to accomplish their work as expertly as possible. They knew that a well-maintained lodge was essential to the happiness of their families; they knew that their work was every bit as important as that of the men. The women even had their own societies in which they advanced according to their competence as lodge keepers.

Since the men reserved their energies for hunting and war, during quiet times they sat around repairing or making weapons, gambling, relating accounts of coups earned, or, one of the favorite pastimes, discussing the affairs of their nation and others.

Seated in one of the largest lodges in the camp, in the position of honor to the left of the owner, was Nate King, his legs crossed in front of him. He had just taken his turn at the pipe offered by Broken Paw, and now he solemnly regarded the renowned chief and the four other elders who were waiting to hear his words.

"I thank you for honoring me by agreeing to this meeting," Nate said in barely accented Shoshone. He had mastered the musical tongue well, although nowhere near as well as his wife had mastered English. "The words I have to speak are important not only for the people of Broken Paw, but for all Shoshones."

"You have us very curious," the venerable chief responded. He was an older warrior who had counted over 40 coups in his lifetime. Beyond him hung over a dozen scalps, trophies of his prowess. "I was very surprised when I was told you had arrived in camp since you never pay us a visit so early in the season. I knew you must have a good reason."

"And you are right," Nate said, choosing his words carefully, "proving the wisdom of Broken Paw is as great as everyone says." He paused. "I am here to ask you to consider a proposal I am about to make, and if in your wisdom you agree, then perhaps you will see fit to go with me to Pah da-hewak um da to help convince him to see things our way." Nate waited for a response to gauge Broken Paw's allegiance to the high chief Mighty Thunder in Sky.

"This must be a grave matter indeed," Broken Paw said, "for you to make such a request. If I accept what you say, I will do all I can to help you. And Mighty Thunder in Sky will do the same. His heart is as big as a mountain, and all he cares about is the welfare of our people."

There were murmurs of assent from the other elders. One, Lame Elk, commented, "Mighty Thunder in Sky is a better man than that hotheaded brother of his, Dog with Horns. He always goes around spitting fire."

Nate grinned at the colorful description of Moh woom hah. He had never met the man personally, but all the stories he had been told corroborated Lame Elk.

"Give us your words, Grizzly Killer," Broken Paw urged.

So Nate did. In painstaking detail he related the visit to his cabin by Two Owls and their long talk. He even told about the attempts on the life of the Ute chief and himself. Finally, he concluded, "As an adopted Shoshone, I take great pride in my new people. I know the way of the warrior, and how we live to count coup. But there are times, such as now, when warriors must put the good of everyone above their hunger for glory. Bow Valley is special to the Shoshones. For many generations our people have gone there to make bows and commune with the Great Mystery. Is it not fitting that we be free to do so again? I believe we should accept the Ute offer and try to set up a truce." He gave a slight shrug. "If the truce cannot be worked out, it will be through no fault of ours. And then we will show the Utes why the Shoshones are considered the bravest fighters in the mountains."

A pregnant silence attended the speech. Broken Paw bowed his head in deep thought for several minutes, then grunted and declared, "You always speak with a straight tongue, Grizzly Killer. We will talk over what you have said and give you our decision in the morning."

"I thank you," Nate said, rising. "I am staying with Winona's uncle, Spotted Bull. Send someone to get me at any time." He made his way from the lodge, being careful not to violate proper etiquette by stepping between the warriors and the fire, and inhaled the crisp air once he was outside. The meeting had gone well, he reflected. Now if only they would agree with him!

Nate headed toward the north side of the village, and saw a pair of familiar faces coming toward him from that direction. One was Spotted Bull himself, the other Spotted Bull's son, Touch the Clouds, who qualified as the single biggest man in the entire tribe. A strapping six feet, ten inches tall, Touch the Clouds had been blessed with an awesome physique and a noble mien. Some felt that one day he would be the chief of chiefs since, although he was still a young man, his feats in battle were legendary. Which in itself wasn't surprising. Touch the Clouds was twice as strong as most men. His war club was three times the size of those carried by his fellows, and his stout bow could outshoot any other. In addition, his lance was akin to a sapling. Rare was the enemy who could stand up to so fearsome an adversary.

"Greetings, friends," Nate hailed them.

"How did your talk go?" Spotted Bull inquired. An older, dignified warrior, whose hair bore rare streaks of gray, he ranked in importance only behind Broken Paw himself.

"Fine. I think they will see the benefit to be had from a truce."

Touch the Clouds folded his brawny arms across his massive chest and remarked, "Winona has told us about the theft of your horse. Do you think those two Utes followed you this far?"

"I doubt it. They would not risk running into a Shoshone hunting party."

"She also told us about the missing parfleche," Spotted Bull said. "Taking that was a strange thing to do."

"The whole incident was unusual," Nate admitted. "I have no idea what to make of it. But since my family is safe now, those two no longer concern me." He patted his stomach and continued. "What does matter is the statement you made last night about being short of food. I would like to go out hunting and perhaps bring you back a deer or an elk."

"A fine idea," Touch the Clouds said. "Sitting around doing nothing bores me so much I want to scream. I will go with you."

"And I as well," said Spotted Bull. "We will make a competition of it and see who can drop the first animal."

Within an hour the three of them were heading westward, Zach an addition to their plans, riding proudly beside his father. This was the first hunt he had ever gone on with other warriors and he wanted to prove himself to them.

Because elk and deer invariably came out to graze during the early morning and evening hours and stayed secreted in thickets the rest of the day, the four made for the forested slopes of an adjacent mountain. By moving along the tree line and examining all the game trails leading up from the low meadows, they were soon able to find a trail bearing fresh elk prints.

"What do you say?" Touch the Clouds spoke. "Our wives will make a new shirt of the hide of the first animal killed for whoever brings it down?"

"Let it be so," Nate said, hoping Winona wouldn't give him a piece of her mind over the extra work if he was the one who lost.

They ascended the slope, which was not very steep, and shortly separated when the game trail did the same, one branch bearing to the south, one to the north. Nate and Zach took the south fork, Nate in the lead with the stock of the Hawken braced against his thigh.

The game trail wound among the thickly clustered pines and down into a gully where a creek gurgled. From his vantage point on the crest, Nate spotted three black bears lumbering up the creek toward him. He was inclined to let them pass unmolested. Although not as formidable as grizzlies, black bears could be fierce when they wanted to be. Quite often they traveled in bunches of from two to five in number, and the instant they set sight on a man they might charge. But Touch the Clouds had not specified what kind of animal must be slain to win the shirt, and Nate wanted to spare his wife the long hours of labor required to make such a garment.

"Stay quiet," Nate whispered to Zach. Dismounting, he ground-hitched the stallion and crept partway down the gully to a large boulder, where he crouched and cocked the Hawken. Waiting expectantly, he presently heard the splash of heavy paws in the shallow water.

Peeking out, Nate observed the first bear go by below. The second shuffled in its wake. By far the biggest, the third bear stopped to quench its thirst, giving Nate the chance to take precise aim before firing. At the blast the bear staggered to one side, its head and shoulder slumping low to the ground, its hind end elevated. The other two bears whirled. Then the first one dashed back to sniff at its shot companion. Growling hideously, it turned to scan the gully.

Nate was hurriedly reloading, keeping one eye on the three beasts as he did. He was confident the untouched pair would soon wander off. But he'd reckoned without his horses, one of which suddenly whinnied.

Needing only that sound to focus its fury, the first bear sprang up the slope, moving incredibly fast for so bulky a creature.

The Hawken was not quite ready. Nate had poured black powder down the barrel, but had not had time to insert the lead ball. Yet he dared not let the bear reach his horses—or his son. Throwing caution aside, he gripped a pistol, yanked it out, and stepped into the open, directly in the path of the onrushing brute. He pointed the pistol at its head and fired when the bruin was less than 15 feet away.

Tumbling end over end, the bear crashed to earth, its momentum carrying it forward, upward. Nate thought for a second that he would be bowled over, but the beast came to rest almost at his very feet. He looked down at the blood oozing from the neat hole in its skull, and exhaled in relief that turned out to be premature.

The bear's eyes, which had been closed, blinked wide, and it came off the ground in a scrambling surge of bestial wrath, its enormous jaws gaping wide to seize the thing that had brought it such agony.

Nate saw the bear's tapered teeth. He saw saliva dripping from its mouth and the gleam of savagery in its dark eyes. And he threw himself to the right, next to the boulder. To his rear was a loud snap as the bear's teeth crunched onto empty air. Then he was darting around the base of the boulder, temporarily out of the bear's reach, seeking somewhere to conceal himself while he finished reloading the Hawken. It packed a heftier wallop than his pistols and would put the bear down for certain.

On the crest a rifle boomed.

Halting, Nate glanced on high. A cloud of smoke wreathed Zach's head. The boy was already in the act of reloading, as well he should be since the bear had still not fallen and was racing up the gully toward him. Thinking only of his son's safety, Nate ran after the bear, catching it as it tried to negotiate a sheer section. Without a thought to the consequences he hauled off and smacked it on the buttocks with his flintlock to divert its attention from Zach. He succeeded all too well.

Zach witnessed his father's action. He watched, agape, as the bear whirled and delivered a sweeping blow that sent his pa flying. Believing Nate to be gravely hurt, Zach jabbed his heels into his horse and galloped over the rim, forcing the horse to ride straight at the black bear. His mount neighed in fright and attempted to change course, but gravity worked in Zach's favor, causing the horse to slip and slide, right into the bear.

Struck broadside, the beast squalled at the impact and toppled, rolling like a downed tree down the incline.

At the bottom, Nate had come to rest in the creek. Cold water splashed onto his face and drenched the front of his buckskins. Disregarding the sensations, he pushed to his feet and found himself in as bad a fix as mortal man ever conceived of.

To Nate's right lay the big bear he had shot. In front of him stood the burly second bear. And tumbling down the gully toward him was the first bear. Bears, bears everywhere, and he only had one loaded pistol at his disposal. Flashing the gun out, he aimed at the second bear's right eye and fired.

The very next second an avalanche seemed to smash into Nate, sweeping him off his feet and into the brush on the opposite side of the creek. Dazed, he wound up on his back with a heavy weight athwart his legs. Shaking his head to clear the cobwebs, he looked down and discovered with a start the weight was the first bear, lying motionless.

"Pa!" Zach bellowed, bringing his mount to the bottom at a reckless pace.

Nate barely heard. He had drawn his butcher knife and whipped it above his head to stab before the bear ripped him apart. The animal, though, hadn't budged. Cautiously, Nate gave it a hard nudge with the tip of the blade, and the huge head swayed a fraction. Otherwise, there was no sign of life left.

"Pa!" Zach repeated, galloping up in a spray of water and dust. He could see his father's moccasins protruding from under the first bear's neck but not his father's body, and he leaped from the saddle with his knife in hand to do whatever was necessary to save his pa. A calm voice stopped him cold.

"Quit your squawking, son. My head hurts enough as it is."

Zach sped around the bear and beamed. "You're alive! For a while there I thought this she-bear had busted every bone you have."

"It feels that way," Nate admitted. Grunting, he sat up and replaced his knife in its sheath. "What about the second bear? Did it run off?"

"That one dropped flat when you shot it. We got them all. Every last one."

"I was afraid of that."

"Huh? What's wrong, Pa?"

"You'll see in a minute," Nate said, his head cocked as he listened to the drumming beat of swiftly approaching horses. Leaning forward, he gripped the dead bear by its ears and raised the head high enough to pull his legs free. His ribs aching abominably, he stood.

Spotted Bull and Touch the Clouds raced to the scene with arrows nocked to their bowstrings. The giant gaped at the bear in the creek, the bear by the creek, and the bear a few yards from the creek near Nate and Zach, and declared angrily, "I hate it when you do this."

"It was an accident. I didn't mean to kill all three."

"You always say that," Touch the Clouds complained. "Remember the time you killed two grizzlies? And one of them, old Silver Hair, was the largest bear ever seen by any man living? You said that was an accident also."

"When an animal is trying to tear you to pieces, does it matter how your life is saved?"

"That is not my point." Touch the Clouds slid his arrow into the quiver on his back, then explained. "When I was a boy, I looked forward to the day when I would be known as the greatest hunter and warrior in the whole tribe. The people of our village now see me as the most fearless warrior, but they see you as the best of hunters. So only half my dream has come true."

"Are you angry at me over this?"

"No. I will always be happy to number you among my best of friends," the giant answered, and again he surveyed the dead bears. "But I still hate it when you do this."

Nate and Zach set to work butchering the three carcasses while Spotted Bull and Touch the Clouds went back for pack animals. When the two Shoshones returned with four horses in tow, Spotted Bull dismounted and came over chuckling.

"You should have seen what my son did."

"What?" Nate asked, pausing to wipe blood, gore, and fat off his forearms by rubbing them on the grass.

"He rode among the lodges shouting, 'Grizzly Killer has done it again! Grizzly Killer has done it again,' and then he would not tell them what you had done. So now everyone is waiting for us to show up so you can tell your tale."

The giant's deed, which would be regarded as silly or childish by most whites, was actually fraught with significance, and Nate glanced up at him to say sincerely, "Thank you. A third of this bear meat is yours." He knew that Touch the Clouds had done him a fine favor by announcing the news.

Performing a brave exploit was only part of the way a warrior earned recognition for his valor. If he told no one and had no witnesses, he would never achieve the notoriety he sought. Therefore every warrior was expected, even encouraged, to become an orator of sorts, to regale the tribe with tales of his daring. A particularly notable feat would have to be told and retold endlessly until everyone had heard the news. In this way fame was spread.

The warriors considered this so crucial that when a war party came back successfully, they would not permit any single brave to ride on ahead and perhaps spoil everything by letting it be known what they had done before they got there. The warriors enjoyed the public recognition their courage garnered them, and they would fly into a rage should anyone presume to deny them their due.

Touch the Clouds, by advertising Nate's accomplishment, had aroused interest to a fever pitch. He had, in effect, enhanced Nate's prestige by making Nate the topic of every tongue. The Shoshones would swamp Nate with requests to hear of the killing of the three bears, keeping him busy going from lodge to lodge until each and every person knew the facts. It was rare for one warrior to do such a thing for another, simply because competition for high honors was so intense. The giant had shown not only the depth of his friendship, but the magnitude of his humility.

"I am grateful for your offer," Touch the Clouds responded sincerely.

Nate pointed at the bear in the creek. "There is the meat you can have. You will notice it is still wrapped inside a hide, so you might as well have both."

"You are giving me the *whole* bear?"

"I cannot give you all three because Winona will want one and the other is Spotted Bull's."

"Mine?" the venerable warrior blurted out. He blinked and covered his mouth with his hand, which was the Indian way of expressing amazement.

Hunters quite frequently shared their spoils. Giving away entire bears, however, had never been done before, and before long stories of Nate's generosity would be circulating along with those of his hunting prowess.

"There was a time," Touch the Clouds said, his voice oddly strained, "when I thought all whites were worthless, more like animals than men, only interested in drinking and fighting and filling their pockets with the strange metal they seem to worship." He advanced and placed his huge hand on Nate's shoulder. "You have shown me different, Grizzly Killer. There are whites who have the heart and spirit of an Indian. There are whites who are in every way our equals."

The next several hours were busy ones. The meat was wrapped inside the hides and tied onto the packhorses. All the claws and the tails were stuffed into a parfleche. Using tomahawks, Nate and Touch the Clouds cracked the skulls of all three beasts and removed the brains so their wives could use them to make the paste so essential to treating skins.

They were a gleeful foursome as they headed down from the mountain, and Spotted Bull started them singing. Nate, riding in the lead, gazed out over the pristine valley and saw the two blue-green forks of the stream sparkling in the bright sunlight and gray ribbons of smoke rising from many of the lodges. At times such as this he was profoundly thankful he had mustered the courage to leave New York City years ago and venture to the frontier. He shuddered to think how his life would have turned out had he stayed: years spent chained to a desk at an accounting firm, poring over heavy books hour after hour, day after day. Sometimes, he reflected, a person had to take risks in order to gain greater rewards.

Nate picked up the pace once they reached the flatland. He was surprised to see a lone rider galloping toward them when they were still over a mile from the village, and his surprise changed to consternation when he presently recognized the rider as his wife.

"That's Ma, Pa!" Zach exclaimed simultaneously.

"I know."

"What the dickens could she want?"

"We'll soon find out," Nate said, feeling his stomach muscles involuntarily tighten. Winona would not be coming to meet them unless she had a very important reason, and something told him he wouldn't like hearing what it was.

Her long hair flowing, her supple body molded to her mare as if she had been born in the saddle, Winona applied her quirt furiously. She met them in a field of grass, reining up so sharply her horse slid a few feet, and announced urgently in Shoshone, "I thought you should know right away, my husband. Something unusual has happened."

"What?" Nate responded.

"Dog with Horns has just arrived in our village. And I was told he has been asking about you."

Chapter Seven

Every man, woman, and child had turned out to see Moh woom hah, or Dog with Horns, one of the most noted Shoshone warriors and brother to Mighty Thunder in Sky himself. Even Chief Broken Paw, Lame Elk, and the other elders were on hand, as the unwritten protocol of their people demanded, to honor the illustrious brave.

Nate saw the throng packed together at the center of the village when he rode in from the north. Making for Spotted Bull's lodge, he tethered his horse and helped strip the hides, meat, and parfleches off the pack animals. Next he checked to be sure all of his guns had been reloaded, and only then did he head for the scene of all the fuss, his son and wife by his side. Winona's uncle and Touch the Clouds followed.

Fifteen warriors were included in Dog with Horns's party. They were all laughing and joking with Broken Paw's people, some embracing relatives or friends they had not seen since the last gathering of the entire tribe. At the very middle of the crowd stood Dog with Horns himself, conversing with Broken Paw and Lame Elk.

Nate studied the man as he made his way through the Shoshones. The hothead was exactly as described: a short, stocky individual whose bronzed physique rippled with layers of muscle. Dog with Horns stood with his shoulders squared and his chin jutting out defiantly at the world, the very picture of human arrogance. He had a bullet pouch and powder horn slung across his broad chest, and clutched in his right hand was a rifle. But it wasn't one of the typical cheap trade rifles the Indians received in exchange for beaver pelts. It wasn't a fusee. No, this was a genuine Hawken, almost a virtual copy of Nate's own gun. And it gave Nate food for thought.

Indians rarely owned Hawkens. Not only were the rifles manufactured by the Hawken brothers of St. Louis much more costly than trade guns, they were difficult to come by for the simple reason there wasn't a trapper alive, free or company man, willing to part with his prized possession no matter how much he was offered.

So there were only three possible explanations for Dog with Horns having one. Either the warrior had somehow been able to afford its purchase price, or he had found a rare mountain man willing to trade it away, or he had stolen the gun.

Nate had no proof one way or the other, but a hunch told him the third possibility was the most likely. There was something about the warrior, perhaps Dog with Horns's transparent arrogance or another quality less obvious, that Nate instinctively didn't like. He suppressed his feelings as he came close to the special guest and waited to be properly introduced.

Chief Broken Paw had about run the gamut of notable braves in his village, and was turning to lead their distinguished visitor to his lodge when his eyes alighted on the returned hunters. "Ho!" he declared. "Here are some men you must meet, Dog with Horns. One of them is the man you asked for."

The brother of the high chief smiled as the introductions were made, but the smile did not light up his dark eyes. He stared at Nate the whole time, and when Broken Paw stopped talking, he said, "It is my pleasure to meet these three. Touch the Clouds, it is rumored, might one day be a chief himself. Spotted Bull's many coups are a credit to his family and all Shoshones." He paused. "As for Grizzly Killer, what need be said?"

And that was it. No compliment. No acknowledgment of Nate's status in the tribe. Just a statement so phrased that it could be construed as a flattering comment or as a blatant insult. Nate had the feeling it had not been the former. Nonetheless, he stepped forward and said, "It is my pleasure to welcome Dog with Horns to our village. Perhaps he will do me the honor of visiting my lodge during his stay?"

"You can be sure I will look for you," Dog with Horns responded. "I have already agreed to stay with Broken Paw. Know, though, that seeing you is one of the purposes for my being here."

Touch the Clouds came forward. "Would you accept an invitation to my lodge to eat tonight? Grizzly Killer killed three black bears earlier and we have enough fresh meat for a feast."

"Three bears?" Dog with Horns said. "Then what they say is true? He kills bears like other men kill flies?"

"He claims he does it by accident," Touch the Clouds mentioned, which sparked laughter in everyone listening except for the guest of honor.

"A man should never be shy about his skill," Dog with Horns said. "At least, an *Indian* should never be."

Although the sky was clear, clouds marred the features of some of those present, Nate among them. He had just been insulted, but again Dog with Horns had done it in such a way that it seemed perfectly innocent. Unwilling to let the slur pass unchallenged, he said, effectively turning Dog with Horns's own words against the man, "As an adopted member of the tribe, I thank you for your kind regard."

"You have a nimble tongue," Dog with Horns countered. "That is good to have when prying into matters better left alone." Before Nate could reply, the warrior motioned and Broken Paw led him off, many of the village's inhabitants trailing devotedly.

Touch the Clouds faced Nate. "You have never met him before?"

"Never."

"Odd that he should dislike you so."

"You noticed, did you?"

"What did he mean about coming here to see you?"

"If I knew that my heart would not be so troubled," Nate said. He rotated on his heel and began to retrace his steps to Spotted Bull's lodge, but he hadn't gone ten feet when the man himself appeared at his right elbow.

"There can only be one reason Dog with Horns has come. He has heard that you are pushing for a truce with the Utes. I have heard he despises them, so I would not be surprised if he wants to stop you before you can convince too many others to agree to the idea."

"That was my first guess, but we must be wrong," Nate said. "How could he have learned about the visit of Two Owls to my cabin? I have told no one except for Broken Paw, a few of the elders, Touch the Clouds, and yourself."

"My tongue speaks true. Dog with Horns knows."

Logic dictated Spotted Bull must be mistaken, but Nate didn't debate the point because his intuition was telling him the same thing. Somehow, some way, Dog with Horns had learned of the peace plan. If so, then Nate had to marvel at how swiftly Dog with Horns had reached the village. He tried to figure the time involved: Since it would have taken Dog with Horns three days, riding almost night and day, to make the trip from the east fork of the Snake River, Dog with Horns had to have learned of the matter at least four days ago. Yet at that time Nate and his family had still been en route from their cabin and no one else had even known of their mission. To make the matter more puzzling, since his family had only been in the village a single day, there hadn't been time for anyone to ride to the Snake and inform on them. So how in the world had Dog with Horns heard, if indeed he had? It was all totally perplexing.

Nate spent the rest of the afternoon trying in vain to make sense of the mystery. And there was another aspect worthy of his attention, a far more disturbing one. Assuming Dog with Horns did know, his rushed trip to Broken Paw's village and his hostile attitude toward Nate indicated he most definitely was opposed to smoking a pipe with the Utes, as Spotted Bull had said might be the case.

Nate didn't relish the notion of having so prominent a brave as an enemy, especially one who had the ear of Mighty Thunder in Sky himself. Dog with Horns could cause him no end of trouble in a variety of ways. Among them was speaking against him behind his back, which would cause ill will toward him in the other Shoshone villages. Those who didn't know him personally would easily be swayed by the opinion of a warrior who ranked so high in the councils of their nation. Or

Dog with Horns might go even further and try souring the Shoshones on the notion of adopting whites into their tribe; he might try to have Nate stripped of any tribal affiliation and made an outcast.

As the time neared for the feast, Nate tried convincing himself he was making a mountain out of the proverbial molehill. He had no real proof Dog with Horns was against the truce. For all he knew, there might be another reason for the warrior's arrival. Yet despite rationalizing the situation over and over, he was still wary as he neared the lodge of Touch the Clouds.

This was an informal affair, so wives and children were permitted to attend. Winona, as was the custom, had brought the bowls and spoons they would need to eat with.

Nate gave his wife's arm a gentle squeeze as they paused outside the flap; then he smiled at Zach, stroked Evelyn's brow, and stooped to enter. Everyone was already there. The men were seated in a ring toward the back, the women were busy preparing the food, and the children were playing quietly.

Nate moved to the right and stopped, waiting for the giant to indicate where he should sit, while his wife and son separated and joined their respective groups. A discussion had been taking place among the warriors when Nate entered, but now it had stopped and all eyes were on him. He was bothered by the steady, almost hostile stare of Dog with Horns, yet he did not let on.

"Grizzly Killer!" Touch the Clouds declared with a broad smile. "Come, my friend. Join us."

The place saved for Nate turned out to be to the right of the giant. Occupying the guest place on Touch the Clouds's left was Dog with Horns. As Nate sank to the ground, he nodded at Spotted Bull, who was on his right, and at the other Shoshone leaders present: Broken Paw, Lame Elk, and four more.

To the left of Dog with Horns sat three braves who had arrived with him. All three were studying Nate intently.

"You are just in time," Touch the Clouds said. "My belly has been growling and I was about ready to start eating without you."

"Maybe the reason he was delayed is because he had to kill another bear on the way here," Dog with Horns commented, a fake smile plastered on his smug features.

And that statement set the tone for the whole evening. From then on, Dog with Horns took advantage of every opportunity to make remarks either about Nate or white men in general, remarks that, while not open insults, left no doubt as to his animosity.

Nate was given a partial reprieve during the main course of the meal when everyone was too busy eating to talk. Touch the Clouds's wife had outdone herself, and the food was outstanding. Served up first was a huge tin containing juicy stewed bear meat. Then came a slightly smaller pan filled with roasted deer. There was also a boiled flour pudding, a tangy sauce made from sugar and berries, and plenty of strong, sweet coffee. For dessert they were fed delicious cakes.

Despite the undercurrent of bad blood, Nate ate heartily. Indeed, it was always expected of guests at a meal that they would eat every last morsel placed before them. Not to do so was a supreme insult. So he filled his stomach to bursting, then sat back contentedly and waited for Dog with Horns to broach the subject he felt sure had brought the warrior to the village. Nor was he kept in suspense for long.

Chief Broken Paw had just given an account of recent events: telling of a man who had been gored while on a buffalo hunt, of the coup certain warriors had earned on a recent raid against the Sioux, and of the ongoing depredations of the Blackfeet, who were getting bolder and bolder all the time.

"When a nation is as powerful as ours," Dog with Horns said, "it can expect to have powerful enemies. The Blackfeet, the Bloods, the Piegans"—he glanced sharply at Nate—"the Utes, they are all worthy fighters. We must always be strong as a people if we are to hold our own against them."

"Very true," Broken Paw agreed.

"How about you, Grizzly Killer?" Dog with Horns asked. "Do you agree?"

"No true warrior would not."

"Ahhh," Dog with Horns said, propping his elbows on his knees. "I am pleased to hear you share my sentiments, but I am confused by your words since your actions go against them."

Nate stiffened. He had just been branded a liar in front of the leading men of the village, an insult so grievous that normally bloodshed would be the likely outcome. But he wasn't about to let resentment cause him to do something he would later regret. Not since he half suspected he would be playing right into Dog with Horns's hands if he did. To buy time to collect his thoughts, he slowly lowered his coffee, aware that all activity in the lodge had ceased and everyone had turned toward the men to better hear his response. "Perhaps I can correct your confusion if you would speak plainly and not in riddles such as young children use."

Someone gasped. One of the visiting braves made a move as if to grab his knife, but the man next to him stopped him.

Dog with Horns was unruffled. Nodding, he spoke softly but with an edge to his tone. "You have a point. A true man does not hide his intentions behind clever words. Very well." He leaned forward. "It has come to my attention that you plan to push for a truce with the Utes over Bow Valley. It is said you will visit my brother soon and try to persuade him to smoke the pipe of peace. Is all this true?"

"It is," Nate said.

"Then it is good I came, so I can show you how wrong you are before you make a fool of yourself in front of the whole tribe."

"That is the reason you have come here?"

"None other."

Nate looked into his tin cup and gave the coffee a swirl. "Now it is my turn to be confused. Since I have told so few, and none of them could have let you know, how is it you have learned all this?"

"How I learned is unimportant," Dog with Horns said. He chuckled, then added, "But you might say a snake told me."

The three members of his band all laughed.

"I did not know you are gifted with the power to talk to animals," Nate responded. "If I had that gift, perhaps I would ask the same snake why you are opposed to a truce."

"The answer is simple. It is not best for our people."

"How can saving lives be wrong for them?"

"Heed what I say next. Since you are white, I do not expect you to fully understand, but I will make this as simple as I can to make it easy on you." Dog with Horns made sure everyone was paying attention to him before going on. "Our people are a warrior race. We live to fight, to count coup. Because we are strong, our enemies fear us and make fewer raids on us than they would if they thought we were a nation of cowards." He glanced at Broken Paw and the other leaders of the village. "Which they will do if they hear we are making peace with our enemies instead of taking their scalps. The Blackfeet, the Bloods, the Piegans, they will say the Shoshones are like women, and they will feel free to come and take from us whatever they want. Our horses, our weapons, our wives and children, they will take them all. We will be laughed at by every tribe in the mountains and on the plains."

"You are exaggerating," Nate said.

"Let me finish, white man," Dog with Horns responded testily. "There is another reason why I do not want a truce. Our dispute with the Utes is an honorable one. Bow Valley should be ours, not theirs, and eventually it will be if we do not show weakness now."

A long silence followed this declaration. Nate knew every person present would be hanging on his every word, so he had to choose each one with the utmost care. Of critical importance was winning over Broken Paw. He needed the chief at his side when he went before Mighty Thunder in Sky to lend weight to his proposition. Unfortunately, he couldn't determine from the chief's expression whether or not Broken Paw had been swayed by Dog with Horns's argument.

Lifting his head, Nate locked eyes with the distinguished visitor and said, "As an adopted Shoshone, as a hunter of note and a man who has counted many coups, I know the importance of being strong in the face of our enemies. When the Blackfeet attack, am I not one of the first to help drive them off? Whenever a Shoshone is in need of help, have I not been willing to lend a hand? Is there anyone here who would question my bravery?"

For a second Dog with Horns appeared on the verge of accepting the gauntlet. His lips parted, then closed again. Evidently he realized how unseemly it would be to criticize Nate's widely known past achievements.

"So when I say that establishing a truce with the Utes has nothing to do with courage or the prowess of the Shoshones in battle, I hope all here will see the truth,"

Nate went on. "Think. Remember our triumphs. For every time the Blackfeet have made a successful raid on us, we have made one on them. For every Shoshone scalp the Bloods have taken, we have taken one of theirs. There is not a tribe anywhere who regards us as weak." He took a sip of coffee. "Dog with Horns would have you believe that if we make peace with the Utes, then other tribes will think they can do as they please with us, but a little thought should show you how wrong he is. When the Blackfeet made peace with the Piegans, did anyone think that of them? Of course not. And when the Cheyennes made peace with the Arapahos, did any other tribe go into Cheyenne territory and try to take what they wanted? No, because the Cheyenne are strong just as we are strong."

One of the village elders grunted, a sign of agreement.

"Instead of showing us as weak, a truce would show we are powerful. For only a powerful tribe, one that commands much respect, can force an enemy into making peace. This is how the Blackfeet will think. They will say among themselves, 'The Utes smoked the pipe because they were afraid of the Shoshones.'"

"This is true," Broken Paw commented.

Delighted, Nate drove home a few more points. "If we do make peace with the Utes, it will free us to pay more attention to our enemies to the north and the east. Our women and children will be able to sleep a little easier at night. And our warriors will once more be able to carry bows made from the special wood in Bow Valley. Is all this not worth the effort?"

Again silence ensued. Since Dog with Horns had been the one who challenged Nate, he had to be the one to again offer an opposing viewpoint.

"Your tongue is like a spider's web," the renowned brave began, "and like the strands of a web, the statements you have made will trap our people in a position where they will come to great harm. I can see that, and so can anyone else who sincerely cares for our nation. But even if I am wrong, even if our enemies do not decide we are weak enough to be destroyed or driven from our lands, there is one more reason for not making peace. And it is this." He jabbed a finger at the men from the village. "How many of you know someone who lost a loved one to the Utes? How many of you lost a relative or a friend yourselves? I did. And I refuse to let the deaths go unavenged. Their blood cries out for us to do something, to show our love for them by taking the lives of those responsible."

Nate knew he must tread cautiously. It was hard to fight strong personal feelings by appealing to human reason, as his reading of James Fenimore Cooper had shown. So he didn't bother trying. He merely mentioned, "The Utes have lost as many loved ones as we have, which does not excuse their actions at all. Many have ample cause to mourn, to hate. But do we want even more to suffer in the same way? They will. If the Bow Valley issue is not settled, many on both sides will lose their lives, and all because we were not wise enough to end the conflict when we had the chance to do so." He surveyed the ring of warriors. "I ask you. Which will benefit our people more in the winters ahead, revenge or peace?"

The question served as the cue for general talk to resume, with the warriors engaged in earnest conversations over the topic of the truce.

Dog with Horns shifted his attention to Broken Paw. "I would like to know whether you agree with me or with Grizzly Killer?"

"Both of you spoke well," the chief answered. "I have not made my decision yet, but I will say I am leaning in favor of making peace. Bow Valley is a place of much good medicine. It will be good to go there again to seek knowledge of the Great Mystery."

Suddenly Dog with Horns uttered a fierce, "*Wagh!*" and surged erect. With a curt gesture at the trio who had come with him, he stormed toward the entrance, shoving aside a child who accidentally blundered into his path.

"Wait!" Broken Paw shouted, rising. "Why go away mad? Sit down so we can continue to discuss this like grown men should."

"Talk! Talk! I am tired of talk!" Dog with Horns responded. "We nearly rode our horses to death to get here before any of you left to see my brother, and for what? Even after I have made clear why the truce must not come to pass, you favor the white eyes over me!"

"Grizzly Killer is as much our brother as you are," Broken Paw said. "We all respect him highly."

"I see that now. And I tell you to your faces that you are making a grave mistake." Dog with Horns glared at Nate. "Know this, trapper. You have made an enemy here this day. I refuse to sit down with the Utes, and I will do all in my power to convince my brother to do the same. You have been warned!" Wheeling, he strode out, his head held high, his fists clenched at his sides.

For the third time that evening total quiet prevailed in the lodge.

"I am sorry the feast had to end like this," Broken Paw said at length to Nate. "Now you know why some say he is a bit hotheaded."

"A bit?" Nate replied.

Touch the Clouds swung toward him. "What will you do now, my friend? Will you still go ahead with your plan?" he inquired earnestly.

"Yes. I just wish . . ." Nate said, and broke off, unwilling to air his personal worries in public.

"What?" Touch the Clouds prompted.

Nate changed his mind. He saw no harm in baring his soul among close acquaintances. "I just wish I knew how far Dog with Horns is willing to go to stop me."

"There is no telling," Broken Paw said somberly. "No telling at all."

Chapter Eight

He was called The Rattler, and he was a happy man. Happy because there was nothing The Rattler enjoyed doing more than killing. Happy because in a very short while he would kill again, with relish.

The Rattler sat astride his fine pinto on the crest of a spiny ridge overlooking the beautiful virgin country that comprised the headwater region of the Snake River, his thin lips curling in a wicked grin. This was the heartland of the Shoshones, or the Snakes as some called them, and no other Ute had ever penetrated this far into their domain. The audacity of his strategy impressed even himself.

Hoofbeats sounded. Leaping Wolf appeared alongside the pinto, commenting, "I do not like this."

"As you have made clear fifty times since we left our village," The Rattler said, making no attempt to conceal his disgust.

"Some of the others share my feelings."

Twisting, The Rattler surveyed the ten warriors clustered in the clearing behind him. "Cowards," he muttered. "I have brought cowards with me instead of fighters."

Leaping Wolf bristled. "You have no right to call us that. Every man here has proved his courage again and again. Some of us have even counted as many coups as you."

A heavy sigh presaged The Rattler's response. "Are you a woman now that you snap at everything a man says? I have high regard for all of you or I would not have asked a single one of you to come along."

"If only we had known," Leaping Wolf said wistfully.

"What cause do you have to complain?" The Rattler demanded. "Have we lost a man yet?"

"No," Leaping Wolf conceded. "But I have a broken nose and you have a wound in your side from the bullet that creased you."

"Do you hear me complaining?"

"And Bloody Tooth never came back. Do not forget him."

"How can I, when you remind me so often?" The Rattler replied sourly. "I always knew you were too fond of that stupid dog and you have proven me right." He snorted. "No one gives a name to something they might one day need to eat! You should have been born a Comanche. I hear they love their dogs as much as they do their women."

"Bloody Tooth was different than most. He was intelligent and loyal. Had it not been for him, Grizzly Killer would have slain both of us."

At the mention of the white man The Rattler hated most, his features took on the aspect of a storm cloud. "Grizzly Killer!" he snarled. "He has been a thorn in the side of our people for far too long! Over and over we send warriors to kill him, yet each time he sends them on to the spirit world instead. How a white eyes ever acquired such strong medicine I will never know!"

"Perhaps he gets his medicine from his Shoshone wife."

"He was killing Utes before he ever brought her to his strange wood lodge. No, as much as I want to slice his hair from his head, I must admit he is an enemy a man can be proud of."

"I still do not understand why we did not kill him when we had the chance," Leaping Wolf mentioned. "There were just the four of them, and one a boy and another a baby. It would have been so easy."

"Why must I explain my plan again and again?" The Rattler asked angrily. "At first I wanted him put under too. That is why I tried at his lodge and again when he came after us. But later, when I was sitting by the fire tending my wound, a better idea came to me. A brilliant idea that will not only put an end to the mighty Grizzly Killer, but will also put an end to any hope Two Owls has of making a truce with the Shoshones. Be patient. All of you. It is just as well we did not kill the white bastard, because now the Shoshones are going to do it for us."

And with that, The Rattler threw back his head and laughed.

Nate King had only been to the headwaters of the Snake one other time, so he was not as familiar with the region as he would have liked to be. That became evident when he tried to shave a day off their travel time by taking a route he thought would be a shortcut, and instead they found themselves in a maze of narrow valleys covered with timber so thick they could barely get their horses through.

"You and your shortcuts," Winona remarked the morning after as they strapped the last of their parfleches onto their packhorse.

"How was I to know?" Nate grumbled.

Zach, already mounted, gazed at the tangle of vegetation and commented, "It's too bad we couldn't have waited for Broken Paw and the rest, Pa. I bet they know this country real well."

"I'm sure they do," Nate said. "But we couldn't afford to dally until they checked on that report of a Blackfoot war party being close to the village." He made certain the lead rope was securely fastened. "We had to leave right away if we're to reach Mighty Thunder in Sky's village shortly after Dog with Horns does."

"And that's important?"

Nate nodded as he helped Winona into the saddle. She had the cradleboard snug on her back, and little Evelyn was peering out in wonder at the world. "The more time Dog with Horns has to work on his brother, the more likely he just might poison Mighty Thunder in Sky against the truce idea," he said. Lifting an arm, he took Evelyn's tiny fingers in his and gave them an affectionate squeeze.

"How soon, do you reckon, before Broken Paw catches up to us?"

"A few days at the most," Nate answered, glancing around. "Why? Are you nervous about us going into Mighty Thunder in Sky's village all by ourselves?"

"Me? I'm the son of Grizzly Killer. Nothing scares me."

"We talked about being afraid once before, as I recollect. It's perfectly normal," Nate said. "The important thing is to not let your fear get the better of you."

"So you keep telling me. But it's easy for you."

"Where did you get that crazy notion? I've been scared more times than you have hairs, yet not once has controlling it been easy," Nate said.

Zach snickered. "Aww, you have not. You're just saying that to make me feel better."

Moving to the stallion, Nate swung up and rested the Hawken in the crook of his left elbow. "Son, there hasn't been a man born who hasn't been scared at one time or another. Scared for himself whenever someone else or a wild animal tried to take his life, scared for those he loved any time danger threatened them, or just generally scared he'd live his whole life through and not amount to much."

"I don't understand that last part."

"You will when you're older," Nate said, assuming the lead. "There's something inside of a man that makes him want to be more than he is, makes him want to do things with his life that will count for something. Like this coon, for instance. Back when I was an accountant I always had this feeling there was something better for me somewhere, that I didn't have to spend all my days chained to a desk. And I was right." He admired the striking scenery all around them. "All I had to do was get off my backside and go look for it."

For the next several hours they journeyed through some of the most rugged terrain Nate had ever encountered in all his travels. Toward noon they climbed a low knoll, and drew up in surprised relief on spying an enormous village sprawled out in front of them.

"We found it," Zach said with less than sterling enthusiasm.

"You stick close to your ma," Nate directed. "No matter what happens, you watch out for her and your sister."

"What can happen, you figure?"

"There's no telling," Nate said. "If Dog with Horns has them all riled up, they might not take kindly to our visit."

"Would they try to hurt us, Pa?"

"There's no telling."

"Once they hear who you are, they wouldn't dare."

Nate smiled knowingly and headed down the knoll. Youngsters were naturally so trusting and kind that it seemed a shame to him they had to be disillusioned by the lessons life taught them later on. Learning that other people could be inconsiderate, ruthless, and downright evil was one of the most bitter pills any growing person had to swallow.

There was a sudden commotion in the village with much yelling and running about. Presently a score or more of riders burst from the lodges and swarmed across the intervening open space with more straggling behind.

"Stay calm," Nate said for Zach's benefit. "They don't know who we are yet so they're not taking any chances."

A handsome warrior carrying a lance was at the forefront of the braves. Nate fixed him with a friendly look and called out in his best Shoshone at the top of his lungs so they all would hear, "We come in peace to see Mighty Thunder in Sky. I am Grizzly Killer, from the village of Broken Paw."

Immediately the leading braves slowed. The man bearing the gaily decorated lance brought his fine sorrel right up in front of the stallion and frankly studied the newcomers for a moment. "I am Long Holy," he declared. "I have heard of you."

"I come to speak with Mighty Thunder in Sky about a most urgent matter," Nate said.

"You come at a bad time."

"Why?"

"Mighty Thunder in Sky is mourning the death of a close member of his family killed by unknown enemies."

"I am sorry to hear of this," Nate said sincerely. "When did it happen?"

"The bodies were found one sleep ago." Long Holy turned his horse, held his lance above his head, and addressed the gathering braves. "These are friends. We will do our best to make them welcome."

From the manner in which the announcement was so readily accepted, Nate gathered that Long Holy must be a warrior of some standing. While the other warriors raced back to spread the news, Long Holy escorted Nate and his family in.

"Did you see sign of any hostile war parties on your way here?"

"No," Nate answered. "Is that how Mighty Thunder in Sky lost his relative?"

"Yes. We do not yet know which tribe they are from, but we should soon. A hundred men have been out scouring the countryside since the dead were found."

"A hunter claimed he saw a band of Blackfeet near the village of Broken Paw shortly before we left," Nate disclosed. "Perhaps there are more in this area."

"If so, they will live to regret what they have done. Mighty Thunder in Sky will lead a raid into their territory himself."

"Is he off with the others now?"

"No. He is in his lodge, taking neither food nor drink. His wives say he does not want to be disturbed by any-one for any reason and we are respecting his wishes."

The news was profoundly upsetting to Nate, since it meant a delay of days or possibly longer. And every one counted. He must get the Shoshones to Bow Valley by the Rose Moon or Two Owls might think the Shoshones had no interest in peace and give up trying to establish a truce.

Another problem was Dog with Horns. Nate was sure that the firebrand, being the high chief's brother, would be one of the few permitted in to see him, giving Dog with Horns plenty of opportunity to denounce the peace-making effort. By the time Nate got to present his case, the chief's mind might already be made up.

Word that a white man was in the village had spread like a prairie fire and people were converging from all directions, the children to laugh and point and gawk, the women to stand shyly and stare, the few men still in camp to regard the family with either idle interest or noticeable suspicion.

Long Holy finally halted in front of a large lodge near the center of the village. "This is mine," he told Nate. "You and your family are welcome to stay here for as long as you remain among us."

"I am in your debt."

At a shout from Long Holy a pair of women came out. They were introduced as his wives, Smoky Woman and Her Shawl, who welcomed Winona warmly and fussed over the infant. Nate and Zach stripped the horses, then took all of their gear in and piled it to one side.

"Come with me," Long Holy said when they were done. He led them to a nearby lodge even grander than his own around which were gathered small groups of people. "You have said your business here is urgent so I will check and learn if Mighty Thunder in Sky will see you. But do not get your hopes high." Going over to the closed flap, he called out, and a moment later an attractive woman poked her head outside. Speaking softly, they conversed, and Long Holy pointed to where Nate and Zach were waiting. The woman scrutinized them, said something, and closed the flap.

"I haven't seen hide nor hair of Dog with Horns yet, Pa," Zach remarked. "Do you think he's in there right this minute?"

The thought hadn't occurred to Nate, and he stiffened in surprise. If so, he mused, the hothead would probably try to prevail on his brother not to admit them. Nate spent several anxious minutes waiting for the woman to reappear. When she did, she only spoke a few words before vanishing once again.

"I expected this," Long Holy said as he came over. "Mighty Thunder in Sky will not be able to see you until morning. His wife apologizes, but that is the soonest it can be arranged." He paused. "You are fortunate he will see you at all. I have never seen a man so broken by a death."

The remainder of the day was largely uneventful except for one episode. Nate smoked the pipe with Long Holy and several other warriors. He listened to tales of their exploits and assorted recent events of significance, and was besieged with questions about Broken Paw's village and noteworthy incidents there. Indians enjoyed news and gossip as much as anyone, and they sat listening attentively until he happened to mention the fact Dog with Horns had stopped by for a short while. Then all four men became unaccountably solemn.

"How long ago did he leave?" Long Holy inquired.

"Eight sleeps ago," Nate answered. "A sleep before we did."

"How many warriors were with him?"

"Fifteen. Why?"

"I was afraid there might have been more."

Nate was about to ask what Long Holy meant by that when another brave rushed in, interrupting their talk.

"Standing Bull has returned! He found the tracks of twelve horses and followed them to the barren flatland south of here where the trail disappeared."

"How can tracks just disappear?" Long Holy responded skeptically, rising. "I must hear this from his own mouth."

The Shoshones hurried out. Nate, curious, tagged along to where a group of 30 warriors were being badgered for information by an increasing crowd. A strapping warrior in a beaded buckskin shirt came forward to greet Long Holy.

"We tried our best. We lost them."

"So Running Badger told me. How can this be? Little Raven was with you and he is the best tracker in the village," Long Holy said.

Standing Bull beckoned a small brave over. "He does not understand how we lost the trail."

"They were crafty, these devils," Little Raven said. He was a wiry, excitable man, and he punctuated his statements with many gestures. "They tried every trick there is to confuse anyone who might follow them, yet I was able to read the sign right until we came to the flat country to the south where the ground is as hard as rock. There their tracks ended."

"Did their horses grow wings and fly off?" Long Holy said. "I may not be as good a tracker as you are, but I know that even on the hardest of ground horses leave some sign. There should have been scratches and scrape marks to guide you."

"Do you think I do not know that too?" Little Raven said, showing some irritation at having his competence challenged. "I looked and looked. And I tell you that there was not a single scratch anywhere."

"We all looked," Standing Bull said. "None of us could find so much as a partial hoofprint."

"Mighty Thunder in Sky will be very disappointed," Long Holy said. "How will I explain it to him?"

Having heard every word, Nate made bold to step forward and interject, "Perhaps I have an explanation." Much to his surprise, every person within earshot turned toward him.

"You think that you know how they vanished, white man?" Standing Bull asked with marked sarcasm. "Are you a medicine man that you can see events far off?"

"No," Nate answered calmly, facing the tracker. "Tell me. Did these men you were following stop shortly after they came to the flat country?"

Little Raven pondered a moment. "Yes, they did. How did you guess? That was the only time they stopped too. Had they done so sooner, they might have left a footprint by which I could determine which tribe they were from."

Nate nodded. He had experience himself in distinguishing the different types of moccasins worn by men from different tribes by the shapes of the soles and the weave of the stitching. "As I suspected," he said. "They stopped to cut up some of their blankets."

"Why would they do that?" Little Raven asked.

"Once, when the Blackfeet were after me, I threw them off my scent by cutting up a blanket and wrapping each hoof on my horse so there would be no print at all when it put its full weight down," Nate detailed. He nearly laughed at the comical expressions of wonder they wore. Sometimes, he mused, the simplest answers were so obvious it was startling. "The ruse only works on ground as hard as rock. In softer soil there will always be smudges left by the blankets."

Long Holy regained his composure first. "A truly marvelous way of deceiving an enemy. I must remember to use it if ever the need arises."

"This would indeed explain why I could not find sign," Little Raven said.

"Who ever heard of such a trick?" Standing Bull said. "Leave it to a white man to think of it." His eyes narrowed suspiciously. "Perhaps the ones responsible were white themselves. Perhaps this white man was one of them. Who is he anyway? Why is he in our camp?"

Nate reined in his anger at the accusation as Long Holy disclosed his identity to the members of the search party. When Long Holy was done, Nate declared for the enlightenment of all, "My skin may be white but my heart is Shoshone. Let any who doubt it talk to Broken Paw and his people. They know me well and they will vouch for my integrity. I would never kill a fellow tribesman."

"No one claims you did," Long Holy said, casting a pointed glance at Standing Bull.

And that was that. The gathering broke up, and Long Holy conveyed the news to the lodge of Mighty Thunder in Sky. Later another search party returned to also report failure in finding the culprits.

To say that Nate spent an anxious night would be an understatement. He tossed and turned, unable to get comfortable, working and reworking in his mind exactly what he should say when he sat before the chief. So much depended on his eloquence, and he didn't consider himself a persuasive man with words. He wasn't glib, like his closest friend and mentor Shakespeare McNair, who could charm a rattler out of its rattles. If he was to have any hope of convincing Mighty Thunder in Sky, he must rely on simple sincerity.

The sound of a stick being poked into the embers of the fire by Her Shawl brought Nate out of the light slumber into which he had finally drifted in the wee hours of the morning. Easing out from under the blanket so as not to awaken Winona or Evelyn, he donned his moccasins and buckskin shirt and stepped outside. Already a number of men and women were abroad. An elderly woman bearing an armful of limbs smiled at him as she went by. Over by the river several warriors were taking their morning plunge. Although they were naked, they swam unaffected in the frigid water.

Nate went into the bushes, and when he came back he found his son waiting for him. "Morning. What has you up with the chickadees?"

"Can I come with you when you go to see Mighty Thunder in Sky?" Zach asked eagerly.

"Afraid not," Nate responded. "Boys your age aren't allowed to sit in on councils. You know that."

"Darn."

"What's wrong?"

"Oh, nothing much," Zach said forlornly, tracing a line in the dirt with his toe.

"This coon knows better. Talk straight with me."

The boy answered in a rush. "It's just that I don't want to spend the whole blamed day with the women, Pa. Not that I have anything against them or don't like Ma or anything like that. But I'm getting too old to have to follow my mother around like a little kid has to do."

"I see," Nate said, both amused and pleased. This was the first time Zach had ever expressed reservations about being in the company of women, a sure sign he was chomping at the bit to become a full-fledged man. Nate was about to dispense some fatherly advice about patience being one of the prime traits of a grown-up when the lodge flap parted and out stepped Long Holy.

"We can go as soon as we have eaten, Grizzly Killer, if that is all right with you."

"It is fine," Nate said.

"Let us hope Mighty Thunder in Sky is in a better mood than he has been." Long Holy grew somber. "But who can blame him when he is mourning the death of his own brother?"

"Who?" Nate asked, hoping he had heard wrong.

"His brother. Have you forgotten so soon? You told us that you met him when he stopped by the village of Broken Paw. His name was Dog with Horns."

Chapter Nine

The Rattler chuckled as he admired the string of three fresh new scalps tied to a cord looped fast around his muscular waist. "Did you see the looks on the faces of those dumb Shoshones when we sprang our trap? They never suspected."

"They still fought well," Leaping Wolf remarked. "If we had not had them pinned down, they would have killed many of us."

"But they did not," The Rattler said crankily. "When will you learn to look at life as it is and not as it might be or might have been? My plan has worked perfectly and you are just too stubborn to admit it."

"We have been very lucky."

"Luck had nothing to do with it. Thank my spirit guardian, who has watched over me from the moment I first decided to stop Two Owls." The Rattler fondly fingered one of the scalps. "Now, not only have I thwarted him, but I have killed one of the leading warriors in the Shoshone nation and arranged everything so that the Shoshones themselves will slay the white dog who has caused us more trouble than any man alive."

"So you keep saying. But they might not."

"The Shoshones are not complete fools. Once they make the connection, Grizzly Killer will be lucky if they do not throw him to the ground and slice off his hair while he is still alive!"

The interior of the high chief's lodge was cool and gloomy, conditions brought about because he insisted on keeping the flap closed and the fire low, the flames no more than thin flickering tongues lapping at the darkness. Mighty Thunder in Sky's three wives sat by themselves to one side while a pair of small children played near the entrance.

Nate paused upon entering and waited to be bidden to a seat. He had not yet gotten over the shocking revelation Long Holy had made. Dog with Horns dead! The one man who stood in the way of achieving peace with the Utes was gone. Nate should feel elated, since he could now present his case unhindered, yet oddly, he felt terribly agitated, and had to resist a mad impulse to collect his loved ones and ride from the village just as swiftly as their mounts could move.

Mighty Thunder in Sky sat huddled next to the fire, a heavy buffalo robe draped over his wide shoulders, his chiseled features as downcast as it was humanly possible to be and still be alive. A desultory motion was his signal. He hardly bothered to glance up when Nate and Long Holy came over.

Taking his cue from Long Holy, Nate moved to the right of the chief and slowly sank down. Because he didn't care to offend his host by implying Mighty Thunder in Sky couldn't be trusted, Nate had left his Hawken propped against the lodge wall near the entrance.

"Greetings," the chief said in a desultory fashion. "I welcome you. It is an honor to have you as my guest."

To say the esteemed leader of the whole Shoshone tribe was heavy of heart would have been an understatement. Mighty Thunder in Sky's entire body slumped as under a enormous weight. Shadows under his eyes and his stooped posture told of his profound emotional turmoil, of his many hours without sleep or nourishment. He made an effort to square his shoulders that only made the robe slip off on one side. "I have been informed who you are," he said to Nate. "And that you urgently needed to see me."

"Yes," Nate confirmed.

"No doubt you know my only brother has been killed and scalped." Mighty Thunder in Sky hitched the robe back up. "He was found with his hair gone and three holes in his body."

"Bullet holes?"

"No, Grizzly Killer. Arrow holes. Whoever shot him and those with him went around afterward and removed all the shafts."

"I have never heard of anyone doing that before," Nate commented.

"Neither have I. Perhaps they feared we would be able to learn which tribe was involved from the markings on their arrows."

"That could be," Nate admitted, since arrows, like moccasins, were variously made by various tribes. "But enemies usually do not hide the taking of scalps. It is a deed they are proud of."

"There is much about the death of Dog with Horns that puzzles me," the chief admitted. "Why was he coming here? Who would have been brazen enough to attack him so deep in our own country? Why did they work so hard to hide all trace of their identity? Even the lengths they went to in order to avoid being trailed was exceptional."

He stared inquisitively at Nate. "Word has reached me that you saw him just a few sleeps before his death. Did you speak to him?"

"Yes," Nate said.

"Did he give you any idea why he was on his way here?"

This was the moment of truth. Literally. Nate could lie, in which case Mighty Thunder in Sky might become unduly hostile later on when he learned the truth, or Nate could own up to what had really happened and hope for the best. He opted to be frank. "Dog with Horns was going to try and convince you not to agree to establishing a truce with the Utes over Bow Valley."

"What truce? This is the first I have heard of it?"

"I was visited by Two Owls, a Ute chief. He asked me to speak to you on his behalf. If you agree peace would be in the best interests of both tribes, you are invited to a council to be held in Bow Valley during the Rose Moon."

Mighty Thunder in Sky was a study in confusion. "And my brother knew all this? That is why he came to the village of Broken Paw?"

"Yes."

"This makes no sense. How could he have learned that you intended to see me?"

"I asked, but Dog with Horns would not reveal who relayed the news to him."

"What else did he say to you?"

"He was most insistent on not making peace. When he was unable to persuade Broken Paw, he rushed off to come here," Nate hedged. He decided it would be smarter *not* to mention that Dog with Horns had publicly branded him an enemy.

The chief gazed into the fire for a full minute without speaking. Then he suddenly lifted his head and called out, "Food. A lot of food. And hurry." Squaring his shoulders, he threw the robe down and said gruffly, "Enough mourning! I must learn the truth of this matter, and to do so I must be at my full strength."

"If there is anything I can do to help . . ." Nate said, and received a hawkish scrutiny for his overture.

"Later, after I have eaten and washed, we will talk at length about this truce and about my brother."

"Very well," Nate said. Taking the statement as a dismissal, he began to rise.

"Hold, Grizzly Killer," Mighty Thunder in Sky said. "Before you leave I would like your opinion on something." He indicated one of his wives, then nodded toward the side of the lodge where the shadows were dark. "While no arrows or tracks were found at the site of the slaughter, we did find two things that might help us find those who are to blame."

Nate saw the wife pick up a large object and carry it over. She approached from directly behind her husband, so the item she carried was not in clear view until she gave it to the chief.

"Here is one of them," Mighty Thunder in Sky said, holding it up.

Nate stared. And stared. A frigid chill enveloped his body and he barely suppressed a shudder. For suspended by its strap from the chief's weathered hand was a parfleche. Not just any parfleche either. *It was theirs,* the one belonging to his family, the one stolen when the packhorse was taken back on the trail to Broken Paw's village! The implications were staggering.

"Are you all right?" the chief unexpectedly inquired.

"Yes," Nate replied.

"You looked as if a spirit had sat in your lap."

"My stomach has been acting poorly lately," Nate said, since pleading illness was better than the alternative. How, he asked himself, could he possibly explain the situation to the chief's satisfaction?

"This was found near where my brother and the warriors with him were slain," Mighty Thunder in Sky was saying. "It is most peculiar they had it with them since men traveling without wives and children always live off the land as they go. And no other parfleches were found." He set it down and ran a hand over the beads decorating the flap. "Yet this was made by a Shoshone woman. Of that there can be no doubt."

Indian women from one tribe never made anything exactly like the women from another tribe. Styles varied greatly. And within each tribe, every woman took pains to put as much individuality and creativity into every article she produced so that no two were ever the same. If ten women tossed ten parfleches into one big pile, they would have no problem finding their own again later. There wasn't another parfleche anywhere in the Shoshone nation exactly similar to the one the chief was examining, the one Winona had made, the one many of her relatives and friends had seen and would no doubt be able to identify if Mighty Thunder in Sky should take it into his head to have the parfleche taken around from village to village in an effort to identify its owner.

In confirmation of Nate's misgiving, the chief commented, "Long Holy thinks it would be a good idea to have the parfleche shown publicly for every woman in the tribe to inspect. Perhaps that way we could find who made it."

"Doing so would take many sleeps, more than a full moon," Nate mentioned.

"I do not care how long the task takes," Mighty Thunder in Sky said. "Not if I can uncover a clue as to who took my brother's life." The parfleche received an angry smack. "And I will find them! I will take their hair in vengeance! And their wives and children will be taken captive! Everyone will see what it means to tempt my wrath."

A fierce gleam lit the chief's eyes, a gleam that transformed Nate's stomach into a giant knot. Mighty Thunder in Sky wasn't about to listen to the voice of reason, not where the death of Dog with Horns was concerned. Nate thought of Winona and their children and of the fate they might suffer if the chief learned the truth about the parfleche, and he wanted to pound something himself.

"But enough of my personal problems," Mighty Thunder in Sky declared. "Leave me now. Return when the sun is straight overhead and we will talk again."

The fresh air was a tonic for Nate's frayed nerves. As he strode toward Long Holy's lodge he tried to figure out the best course to take. For years he had instructed his son that honesty should be uppermost in all dealings with others, but this time he wasn't so sure. Given the frame of mind Mighty Thunder in Sky was in, the truth might get his family and him slain.

"What is wrong with them?" his companion abruptly asked.

Glancing up, Nate saw Standing Bull, Little Raven, and four other braves a dozen yards to the east, hurrying in the general direction of the chief's lodge. They were conversing excitedly, arguing from the looks of it. Suddenly Little Raven spotted him and whispered to the others, all of whom then adopted flinty expressions. Nate wondered why.

"You go on ahead. I will come later," Long Holy said, turning and hastening after his friends.

Nate did as bidden, his uneasy feeling growing with each step he took. Something had happened, but he was at a loss for an answer until he came within sight of Long Holy's dwelling and saw his wife and son anxiously awaiting him.

"Pa!" Zach declared, running to his side. "You'll never guess who we found right here in the village!"

"Who?"

"Stockings."

Stopping short, Nate looked back. So that explained the attitude of the others! Stockings was the name Zach had given the packhorse that was stolen. "Where did you see him?" he asked.

"Why, tied to a stake near Standing Bull's lodge, of all places," the boy answered. "I couldn't believe my eyes."

Winona came up, Evelyn tucked tenderly in her arms. "Long Holy's wives were showing us around the village," she explained. "When Zach saw our horse he went to pet it. Standing Bull appeared and demanded to know what we were doing with his animal. It seems he took possession of it after Stockings was found near where Dog with Horns was killed." She frowned. "He became quite upset and went off in a rush."

A premonition of grave danger stabbed into Nate's core. "Where are Long Holy's wives now?"

"They left as soon as we came back," Winona said.

Of course they had, Nate reflected. They were off spreading the story to all their friends. By nightfall everyone would know. His more immediate concern, however, was how the high chief would react. "Saddle your horses," he directed. "Forget the pack animal. We'll have to travel light and fast."

"What's wrong, Pa?" Zach asked. "Why are we leaving?"

"I'll fill you in later." Nate stared at each of them in turn. "Trust me on this. And hurry. If we're not gone when Long Holy comes back, we could find ourselves in a heap of trouble."

When a man and a woman have been husband and wife for any length of time, living together 24 hours of every day, doing everything from eating to sleeping together, sharing everything they have and everything they are, an implicit trust builds up between them.

Often the closeness of their sharing results in a bond so deep and so intense they can practically read the other's thoughts. So it was with Nate and Winona. She had only to see into his eyes to know they were in dire straits, and her implicit trust of his judgment and devotion was such that she raced to do as he requested without a word of argument.

Zach brought the horses around. Each of them swiftly threw on their blankets and saddles and climbed up, Nate taking the time to help Winona slip the cradleboard onto her back first. None of the Shoshones paid them much mind, and no one tried to stop them as they applied their heels and made off through the maze of lodges. Not, that is, until they had gone about a hundred yards. Then a harsh shout rang out.

Nate shifted. Standing Bull and a pair of braves were racing in pursuit, the strapping warrior angrily waving a tomahawk. "Keep going," he told his loved ones. "No matter what, don't stop."

Standing Bull continued to bellow. "Grizzly Killer! Hold on! Mighty Thunder in Sky wants to speak with you! Do you hear me?"

Nearby Shoshones were halting to look. Heads were popping out of lodges.

Facing southward, Nate brought the black stallion to a trot. He fervently prayed none of the villagers would take it upon themselves to try to keep him from leaving because the last thing he wanted to do was hurt a fellow tribesman. But he wouldn't let anyone stand in his way. He had a plan, a crazy plan, yet a plan nonetheless to remove the pall of suspicion threatening those who meant the most to him. He would prove beyond a shadow of a doubt that he'd had nothing to do with the death of Dog with Horns, or he would die trying to clear his name.

The last of the lodges was in sight when a lone warrior, having heard Standing Bull's cries, loped at an angle to intercept the fleeing family.

Nate could see the man was unarmed, and he tried a bluff, motioning aggressively with the Hawken, which didn't work; the warrior only ran harder. So Nate waited until the onrushing brave was only a few yards away, then with a jerk of the reins, he rode the black stallion right into the man. The collision hardly fazed the stallion, but the warrior was catapulted backwards to crash down in a daze.

Shortly Nate came to a hill blanketed with trees. He deliberately plunged into the pines to prevent those in the village from seeing his next move, which was to cut to the west for a quarter of a mile. On reaching a creek that fed off the Snake River, he resumed his southward bearing, riding in the middle of the water. The trick wouldn't deceive a skilled tracker like Little Raven unless the sediment had time to settle, but it might slow down a chase party since they would have to proceed slowly in order to find the spot where his family took to solid ground again.

At any moment Nate anticipated hearing the drum of hoofbeats. When half an hour elapsed and there was no hint at all of anyone on their trail, he concluded the Shoshones had wasted five or ten minutes getting a group of pursuers together. Which meant he enjoyed a slim lead, at best. Somehow he must think of a means of losing them.

This was ruggedly mountainous country, with many ridges, ravines, and gorges. The forest in places was so thick that getting a horse through was next to impossible. Boulders of varying sizes were everywhere, posing constant obstacles to speedy progress.

Through it all, the creek wound unhindered by the lay of the land, enabling Nate to cover over five miles swiftly before he called for a halt. Leaving the water, he rode to the top of a spine that jutted from an adjacent peak.

From his lofty perch he spotted a bunch of riders three miles behind, nine or ten in all, coming on rapidly.

Nate raced to the bottom. "They're sure enough after our hides," he announced. "From here on we ride like the wind."

"Why is this happening, Pa?" Zach asked. "What the dickens did we do?"

"They think we had a hand in killing Dog with Horns," Nate responded.

"That's plain silly. We never did no such thing."

"You know that. And your mother and I know it. But the ones who are on our trail think otherwise. Should they catch us, they might not give us the chance to explain ourselves." Nate went up the bank in a flurry of hoofs. At the top he changed course once more, heading to the southeast now.

The morning sun climbed steadily. Other than a few fluffy clouds, the sky was crystal clear and ocean blue. Any other time, Nate would have savored the primeval landscape. Not this day. His whole attention was devoted to the preservation of his loved ones.

Occasionally doubt gnawed at Nate. By running off as he had, his actions tended to confirm whatever suspicions Mighty Thunder in Sky and the rest harbored. The longer he pondered, the more he felt he should have stayed and made a clean breast of the misunderstanding. If they had let him.

There was the stumbling block. Nate had no idea how unreasonable the high chief could be. Mighty Thunder in Sky seemed like a rational man, but the death of a family member had been known to derange the most stable of minds.

A flat stretch between two hills gave Winona the opportunity to ride alongside, and she promptly did so, saying in English, "I hope you have a plan, husband. We cannot spend the rest of our lives as outcasts."

"I do," Nate confided.

"Do you intend to share it before too many winters have gone by?"

"There's only one way of getting to the bottom of this mess, and that's to find the ones who did kill Dog with Horns."

"The search parties lost their trail," Winona noted.

"Hopefully we'll fare better."

"And what will you do if we succeed? I heard there are ten or more, which is far too many for you to handle all by yourself."

Nate gave her his best boyish grin. "I can't help it if the odds are in my favor."

"You are avoiding the question," Winona chided. "Do not make light of such a serious matter. What can we hope to do against so many?"

"I'll admit I don't have every detail worked out yet," Nate said. "As for that 'we' part, once we track the polecats down, Zach and you will hide out somewhere while I deal with them alone."

"We are a family, in case you have forgotten. And aren't you the one who is constantly saying a family should always do things together?"

"I was talking about ordinary things, like chores around the house and going on picnics and fishing and such, not tangling with an enemy war party."

"We are a family," Winona reiterated. "When the time comes, Zach and I will do what we can to help."

"What about Blue Flower? Are you fixing to give her a butcher knife and have her tackle the rascals too?" Nate had played his ace, counting on motherly instinct to keep both Winona and the child out of jeopardy.

"I will hang her cradleboard from a tree where no wild beast can get at it, and she will be perfectly safe and content until we have done that which needs doing."

"Contrary female," Nate muttered.

"I beg your pardon?"

"Don't go talking all civilized on me," Nate said. "You're just trying to get my goat."

"Why husband dearest," Winona said sweetly, her eyes sparkling, "we do not own one."

Seeking in vain for a witty retort, Nate was almost grateful when Zach called his name. Almost, but not quite, for galloping like a demon toward them from the rear was none other than Long Holy, his lance upraised, the point glittering in the sunlight.

Chapter Ten

Nate King's first impulse was to raise his Hawken and take a bead on the warrior's chest. He held the rifle steady, his finger curling on the hammer. Then, with a start, he realized what he was about to do and he jerked the Hawken down to his lap. He couldn't bring himself to fire.

Since Nate was an adopted Shoshone, Long Holy was a fellow tribesman, a member of his wife's people, a man who had shown his family courtesy and hospitality, and Nate wasn't about to put a lead ball into the brave without extreme provocation. So he sat there until the warrior was close enough and raised his hand, calling out, "That's far enough! Why have you chased us?"

Long Holy drew rein. Instead of answering, he rested the lance across his thighs and said, "You were about to shoot. Why did you change your mind?"

"Part of me is Shoshone," Nate said, and let it go at that.

The warrior studied the trapper. "You confuse me, Grizzly Killer. I do not believe you had anything to do with the death of Dog with Horns, yet you fled when we learned that the horse found near where the ambush took place was yours. Why?"

"I am going to find the ones responsible."

"All by yourself?"

"My family will help," Nate said, ignoring the look that spread over Winona's features.

"Just the four of you against a band that killed sixteen seasoned warriors?" Long Holy said incredulously. "Either your brain is in a whirl, or you have more courage than anyone I have ever met."

"I have no choice. In order to show Mighty Thunder in Sky I had no hand in the death of his brother, I must catch those who did," Nate said. "And not just for his sake. I must find the one who stole our horse and parfleche and then deliberately left them at the ambush so I would be blamed. Whoever did this is a devious enemy, a threat to all I hold dear." He hefted the Hawken, his voice lowering. "And I do not take kindly to having those I care for put in danger."

"Would you accept my aid?"

"This is my fight," Nate said, then corrected himself. "*Our* fight." His gaze drifted over the warrior's shoulders. "Where is Mighty Thunder in Sky and those who are with him?"

"Let me ride with you awhile so we can talk," Long Holy suggested. "Otherwise the others will soon be here, and some of them are so angry they might do you harm no matter what I say."

"As you wish," Nate said, conceding the wisdom of not staying there to be caught. The hill to the south offered plenty of cover, so he made for the spruce trees at its base.

Meanwhile Long Holy started speaking. "When I heard

Standing Bull tell Mighty Thunder in Sky about your horse, and listened to some who wanted to have you skinned alive without first hearing your side, I became worried for your safety. I tried to reach my lodge ahead of Standing Bull to warn you, but you were riding off as I got there. So I ran to my fastest war-horse and set out ahead of the rest."

"Why go to so much trouble on my behalf?"

"Because in the short time I have known you, I have grown to respect you, Grizzly Killer. You are not like many whites who think little of our ways and who always speak with two tongues. All the good words spoken of you have proven to be accurate." Long Holy smiled. "I believe I am a good judge of character, so I trust my feelings when they tell me that your heart is true and strong. Your skin is white, but inside you are a brother warrior. And I would not desert my brother in his time of need."

"I thank you," Nate said. An opening in the trees drew him toward it. "And while I appreciate your concern, I urge you to turn around and go back. You risk angering many members of your tribe if you do not."

"So be it," Long Holy said. "You are not the only one who must be true to himself."

Momentarily they reached the hill, and Nate was too occupied with skirting thickets and trunks to indulge in conversation. He did ponder the warrior's offer, though, and admitted to himself that another pair of strong arms would be of definite benefit if and when he overtook the guilty parties. More importantly, there would be someone to escort Winona and the children to safety if something should happen to Nate himself.

Nate did not even consider the possibility Long Holy was lying about wanting to lend a hand. It had been his experience that Indians, more often than not, were ruled by their hearts and not their heads. When an Indian said he liked you, he sincerely did. At least this was true of the Shoshones. Nate had heard some other tribes were not quite so straightforward in their personal dealings; the Crows, in particular, were distrusted by practically all the free trappers. But he accepted Long Holy's declarations at face value.

Beyond the hill the country consisted of more rolling hills broken by intermittent mountains. Nate maintained a swift pace for the better part of an hour. From the crown of a bald hillock he scoured their back trail, and was delighted to see no sign of their pursuers. "We must have quite a lead," he commented in Shoshone.

"Do not expect them to give up and go back," Long Holy said. "Mighty Thunder in Sky will stay on your trail until he gets the answers he wants."

"By the time he has caught up, I hope to have the answers for him," Nate said.

"You mentioned that your horse and parfleche were stolen. Who did this?"

"If I have it figured right, some Utes."

"I recall you saying they seek peace."

"Some do. A few do not." Nate sighed. "There are always those who hate for the sake of hating. Even among the Shoshones there are some who do not like whites. So it is not surprising a small bunch of Utes do not want peace with us."

"There will be more than a few Shoshones who share their sentiments," Long Holy said.

"Dog with Horns was one," Nate said. "He did not want me to come see his brother. And in front of Broken Paw himself he called me his enemy for refusing to go along with him."

"Is that another reason you left the village?" Long Holy asked. "You worried how Mighty Thunder in Sky would behave once he knew?"

"Yes."

"I might have done the same if I were you," Long Holy stated. "You are a wise man, Grizzly Killer, wise beyond the winters you have lived. How is this?"

"A good friend of mine by the name of Wolverine once gave me some of the best advice I have ever received," Nate said, referring to Shakespeare McNair. "He said if I keep my eyes and ears open at all times I might learn enough about life to reach old age without making too big a fool of myself."

"Husband," Winona broke in, pointing behind them. "Look."

A dust cloud framed a gap between two hills through which they had passed some time ago.

"You were right about the chief being persistent," Nate told Long Holy. "How far to the flatland where Standing Bull and Little Raven lost the trail?"

"Two sleeps."

"Damn." Nate squinted up at the sun. "That's more riding than I bargained on," he commented in English, disappointed the sign would be so old when he got there. The older it was, the less chance he would be able to find a clue as to the direction the band had taken. Reverting to Shoshone, he said, "Mighty Thunder in Sky is not the only one who is persistent. We will push our horses until they drop if necessary. No matter what, I am going to catch those who killed Dog with Horns and wring the truth from them."

With that, Nate goaded the stallion into a gallop.

"We should not have stopped," Leaping Wolf protested. "In ten more sleeps we can be back in our own lodges if we keep on going."

"Why are you always in such a hurry to do everything?" The Rattler's temper flared. "There are times when I think you must have white blood in your veins."

"There is no reason to be insulting," Leaping Wolf

said. "I only have our best interests at heart."

The Rattler nodded at the small lake near which they stood. Nestled in a hollow flanked by two ridges and bordered by rich grass, the setting was ideal for grazing their stock and resting. "We have been on the move with little rest and even less food since we left our village. Would you have us ride back looking as if we had been dragged by our horses?"

"No," Leaping Wolf said, his eyes on the northern horizon. "I just do not think we are safe here."

"Are you still worried about the Shoshones finding us?" The Rattler asked. "If so, you should relax. There has been no sign of them. My trick worked. Had it not, they would have been here by now."

"I still do not like it."

Not even trying to conceal his disgust, The Rattler walked to the edge of the lake, stripped off his weapons and his buckskin shirt, and plunged in. The cold water closed over his head, tingling his nose and ears, invigorating him. Using clean, powerful strokes he surfaced and swam parallel with the shore. Several other members of his band were doing the same. One, his wife's nephew and the youngest of them all, was employing an awkward sidestroke that barely kept him afloat. The youth looked around as The Rattler drew near.

"Ho, Uncle! Are you excited about seeing our people again? I am. I cannot wait to hear them sing our praises for the deeds we have done on this raid."

The Rattler slowed to tread water. "You are learning, Holds the Arrows. There is nothing more important in life, nothing at all, than the counting of coup and the glory that comes with it. Remember this and one day you will be as famous a warrior as I am."

"I hope to follow in your footsteps," Holds the Arrows

said. "But after what I have seen on this journey, I do not know how any man could."

The Rattler tried to strike a dignified pose, which was hard to do when up to his neck in water. "After word of this raid is spread, not even Two Owls will dare oppose my wishes."

"There is something I would ask you," Holds the Arrows said. "If it is permissible."

"You need never be shy about approaching me. We are related, are we not?"

"Yes," Holds the Arrows responded. He had to pause when he accidentally swallowed water. Sputtering, he said, "I have been most impressed by the way you have planned out every small detail. You think of everything."

"I try to, but I make as many mistakes as anyone else. The secret is to be adaptable. Adjust your plans as circumstances change." The Rattler began moving slowly toward shore. "Look at how I have done things. At first I wanted Two Owls dead, but when that failed I tried to kill Grizzly Killer. By sheer luck he escaped, and I still planned to kill him until I realized how I could put an end to him, the truce, and my old enemy Dog with Horns all at the same time. By adapting I overcame our enemies. You can do the same."

"You also succeeded because you have no fear. I would never have been able to secretly meet Dog with Horns as you did. I would have feared a trap."

"A good enemy, nephew, is worth more than many bad friends."

"Uncle?"

"I knew Dog with Horns would not have me killed without first hearing why I had come to see him. His curiosity would not let him. That is why I had the woman who was gathering roots take word back to him that I was waiting in the forest."

"You took a great risk."

"Not really." The Rattler glanced around. "No one but you need know this. I met Dog with Horns once, back when we were small children, in the days when the Utes and the Shoshones shared Bow Valley. His people arrived while ours were preparing to leave, and for a day we played together. Or I should say, we fought together, because we were always wrestling or racing or doing something else to prove which one of us was the best. He claimed the Shoshones were superior to the Utes, and I had to show him that was not the case."

"How did you know he would help you try to stop Grizzly Killer?"

"I have studied the nature of men. Beliefs we hold when little often carry over into our adult life. Dog with Horns despised our people when he was young, so I counted on him feeling the same way when I paid him a visit." The Rattler shook his head to clear water from an eye. "The hard part was finding his village. From past raids I knew the general region he would be in, but not the exact spot."

"I hope I am as smart as you are when I am your age, Uncle," Holds the Arrows said.

"Heed my words and do as I do and one day you will be a chief," The Rattler predicted, giving the youth a clap on the shoulder that caused Holds the Arrows to go under. Thrashing and gasping, the young man popped back up.

"Thank you for your time, Uncle."

"One more word, then I must check on my horse."

"Yes, Uncle?"

"Learn to swim."

Long Holy stared in the direction they were heading, to the southeast, and remarked, "You continue to surprise me, Grizzly Killer. I thought you would spend at least a day or two searching for sign."

"And give Mighty Thunder in Sky the time he needs to close in on us?" Nate replied. "This way is better."

"Is it?" Long Holy asked. "What if you are wrong?"

"How can I be?" Nate rejoined. He swept an arm to encompass the rocky ground stretching for miles and miles until it was swallowed by the early morning haze. "If they were Utes, as I suspect, they will certainly not want to stay in Shoshone territory since they know every warrior who can sit a horse will be out after them. Home is where they will head, and just as rapidly as they can. That means they went southeast, and once we reach the end of this wasteland we should find their tracks easily."

Just then Winona rode up next to them and said in English, "Nate, will you please take a look at the right strap. I think the cradleboard is slipping."

Slowing, Nate leaned to the side, giving tiny Evelyn a grin. He also gave the strap a tug, then declared, "Snug as could be, love of my life. And she looks as happy as a lark."

"She will not stay happy if we do not locate water soon. I did not have as much milk to offer her this morning."

"If the Utes crossed this godforsaken area, they must know of someplace to find some."

"Did you stop to think that they do not need water as much as we do? Warriors do not usually bring babies along on raids."

"They have horses, don't they? And horses need regular watering."

"You cannot compare horses to babies."

Nate didn't press the point. He was as worried about the problem as she was, perhaps more so since the blame would fall squarely on his shoulders if harm should befall Evelyn. Crossing the wasteland had been his idea and his alone.

By noon a welcome sight relieved Nate's anxiety. A jagged line of blue-green mounds that grew dramatically in size the farther they went, and by the middle of the afternoon had assumed the towering proportions of regal mountains cloaked in robes of verdant green. Where there was vegetation there had to be water.

Soon the rocky ground gave way to clumps of weeds which in turn expanded into a narrow plain of buffalo grass waving in the wind. Nate was on the lookout for game trails since they invariably led to favorite drinking spots. Temporarily he had forgotten all about the band he was chasing, but he received a timely reminder when he spied brown blotches in the grass, blotches that took on the familiar shape of horse droppings.

"Can I do it, Pa?" Zack asked, eager to demonstrate his skill.

"Go right ahead," Nate told him.

The boy slid to the ground and squatted next to one of the droppings. Touching it, he said, "Pretty hard, Pa." He broke off a small piece and rubbed it between his fingertips, testing the texture. "I figure five, maybe six days."

"That fits," Nate said. He pointed out several sets of tracks. "Here's where they stopped to take the blanket strips off the hoofs of their horses."

"Do you really think we can catch them when they have such a big lead on us?" Zack inquired as he climbed back into the saddle.

"Maybe," Nate said. "It all depends on how badly they want to reach their village. If they're convinced no one is after them, and if they're content to take their sweet time, we have a chance."

From the plain into the mountains they rode, often finding clear hoofprints on patches of bare earth. Steadily upward they bore until, as the sun framed the western skyline, they came to a small lake nestled in a hollow flanked by two ridges. Here they made camp. And here Winona found evidence of a campfire.

"From the amount of charred limbs and such," Nate speculated as he poked the blackened remains with a stick, "they must have rested up a day or two before continuing." His teeth reflected the fading sunlight. "Looking better and better all the time."

Long Holy speared a half-dozen fish for their supper. The night was serene, the stars exceptionally bright. Well before dawn they resumed the chase, and since those they were following had proceeded at a leisurely pace, they were able to gain a lot of ground by nightfall. The next day was the same. And the next.

Finally, the subsequent morning, Nate emerged from a high pass to behold a spacious valley winding southward. And several miles off, near a stream, rose a column of smoke.

"Think it's them, Pa?" Zach asked hopefully.

"There's only one way to find out, son."

Availing themselves of the best cover, they slowly worked their way to the valley floor and into a belt of trees which screened their movements and brought them to within a quarter of a mile of the smoke.

Zach again volunteered, this time to shimmy up a tree. "I see a bunch of horses and some warriors, Pa," he reported. "Can't tell which tribe they belong to from here. Let's see. Eight. Nine. No, there's another. Ten, all told, but there could be more. There's some brush and stuff blocking part of the camp."

"Anything else?"

"Just a big old buck they have strung from a tree limb. Two of 'em are cutting it up."

"That's why they've stopped," Nate said with glee. "All right. Come on down." He leaned the Hawken against a tree, drew his knife, removed his whetstone from his possibles bag, and sat on a log. "I imagine they're tired of eating rabbits and squirrels and such, what with being on the go for so long. They must be fixing to have a fine feast tonight. Then they'll head out come daylight. Well, we'll have something to say about that."

"Do you have a plan, husband?" Winona asked.

"Not yet. I'm sort of making it up as I go along. Give me some time," Nate said. He glanced at Long Holy, and caught the warrior in the act of giving him an intent scrutiny. "Is there something on your mind?" he asked in Shoshone.

"I think you are making a mistake."

"In what way?"

"There are too many. You and your family will be wiped out if you fight."

"Then we will be wiped out together," Nate said, beginning to sharpen his blade.

"Do you value the lives of your wife and children so lightly that you would throw them away for nothing?"

Nate paused in mid-stroke. "There is no one in this world I value more than my family," he said, barely controlling the resentment he felt at having his love for them questioned. "Their lives mean more to me than my own does. And I would not call clearing our name so we can live in peace among the Shoshones again as 'nothing.' "

"I did not mean to insult you," Long Holy said. "I asked because I have grown to like all of you very much and I would not care to see any of you be slain."

"If all goes well we will not be."

"If," Long Holy emphasized, coming closer. "But perhaps there is a wiser way. Perhaps we should wait."

"Wait?" Nate glanced up. "Wait for what?"

"A better chance."

"There will never be a better time. They feel safe here or they would not have stopped, so their guard will be down. And after they fill their bellies tonight, they will be so drowsy we can capture every last one with no problem."

"They might have someone stand guard. I urge you to wait."

The request struck Nate as being so odd that he jumped to the conclusion Long Holy must have an ulterior motive for making it. He thought of how quiet, how preoccupied, the warrior had been the last few days, and for the first time he wondered if he had made an error in allowing Long Holy to tag along. A query was on the tip of his tongue when he detected motion behind the Shoshone, and peering into the trees he saw something that made his blood pump faster.

Zach had been right. There were more members of the band, two more, in fact, and both were coming through the trees straight toward them.

Chapter Eleven

Nate King had only seconds to do something. The Indians were about 30 yards out, talking as they strolled side by side. Neither man was looking in front of him. Soon one was bound to, and all hell would erupt.

"Hide out!" Nate urged, pointing.

Zach and Long Holy glanced around, recognized their plight, and instantly took refuge behind trees.

Winona turned, frowned, and came over to the log as Nate flattened behind it with his rifle at his side.

"Get down here with me! There's room for two."

"You will need a distraction."

"Too risky. Hurry."

As if she hadn't heard, Winona coolly took a seat on the log, adjusted her dress, and began *feeding the baby from her breast*.

"What do you think you're doing?" Nate demanded, grabbing the hem of her garment. "Lie down before they spot you!"

"Shhhhh," Winona said. "And don't miss." She winked at him, then bowed her head, resting her chin on Blue Flower.

The only choice Nate had was to play along. Squabbling would alert the warriors to his presence, and if they attacked, Winona was right out in the open, a perfect target. Furious at the risk she was taking—and not a little proud at her brazen ploy—he rose on one elbow and peeked around her hip.

Both braves were still advancing. The style of buckskins they wore identified them as Utes. Suddenly the tall one on the right, who held a bow, scanned the woods and froze. He had seen Winona and the horses. His companion, gazing in the same direction, blinked in astonishment. Exchanging perplexed expressions, they crouched and came warily nearer, their attitude and posture showing they suspected a trap.

Winona started humming softly while rocking back and forth, her hand gently stroking Evelyn. "Be ready, husband," she whispered. "When they are close enough I will drop down." Then she hummed louder.

Nate could feel sweat forming in his hand, but he dared not release the knife to wipe it off. The Utes were coming on quickly now. They had seen no one besides Winona, so perhaps they believed whoever else was with her had gone on toward the camp. Or perhaps they were concerned for their fellows and wanted to find out what was happening so they could give warning if the other Utes were in danger.

Ten yards out the tall one stopped and used sign to inform the other brave to bear to the left and approach "the woman" from the side.

Pulling back, Nate listened to the tall warrior's almost noiseless approach. The man spoke gruffly to Winona, who simply went on nursing and humming. Sounding angry, the warrior addressed her in Ute once more. The next moment Winona threw herself to the right.

Nate surged to his feet. The tall warrior had a shaft notched to his bowstring, but he was holding the bow at his waist rather than having it ready to shoot. Nate's right arm flashed in a lightning arc. From the end of his hand streaked a glittering bolt that buried itself at the base of the Ute's throat, all the way to the hilt.

Eyes going wide in disbelief, the tall warrior dropped the bow and frantically backed away. Gurgling and whining, he clutched at the knife and yanked it free. In doing so, he transformed his neck into a crimson fountain as blood gushed from the severed arteries. The brave tripped over a root, fell on his backside, and sat there pumping his life's fluid all over the grass.

Nate spun, his right hand falling to his tomahawk. Dispatching the second Ute quietly was imperative if he hoped to avoid alerting the rest. But he need not have worried.

The other Ute stood not eight feet away, his posture unnaturally slumped, his arms and fingers limp. From the center of his chest jutted the explanation, the red tip of Long Holy's lance. Slowly the Ute sank down onto his side. Long Holy placed a foot on the dead man's shoulder, gave a powerful wrench, and tore his lance loose.

From behind a pine Zach stepped. "Awww," he groused, "I didn't get to count any coup!"

"There will be other times," Nate said, watching Long Holy bend over with knife in hand. A few skilled slices and the warrior had his trophy.

"Can I do yours, Pa?" Zach asked. "Please! You've never let me before and I'd love to do it!"

Nate hesitated, inclined to refuse the request. There had been occasions when out of adherence to Shoshone custom he had taken scalps, but he had never been able to reconcile himself to the practice. Like the self-mutilation practiced as a sign of grief, scalping went against his personal grain. Whether done by whites or Indians, barbarism was barbarism. He began to shake his head when Winona nudged him with an elbow.

"Some of the other fathers have let their sons lift hair."

"He's so young."

"My father had his first scalp when he was the same age."

The glow of youthful longing did Nate in. "Go ahead," he said against his better judgment.

Beaming, Zach whipped out his knife, dashed to the tall warrior, and in imitation of the many times he had seen various Shoshones and his father lift hair, he inserted the tip under the front of the scalp, worked the razor-sharp blade back and forth, then straightened with the gory scalp waving from his bloody hand. "Look, Pa! I did it! I did it right!"

"That you did," Nate conceded. "But not so loud. We don't want the others to hear." Since the harm had been done, he added, "You can hold onto it until we get home, if you'd like."

"Thanks, Pa. You're the best father there is."

"Time will tell."

"Pa?"

"Nothing, son. Nothing at all." Turning, Nate moved through the trees to where he could spy on the Ute camp without being seen. From what he could tell, none of them had heard a thing. They were still carving up the buck. A few were seated by the fire. Their horses, he noticed, were tethered near cottonwoods, which gave him an idea for later on.

Zach had fastened the scalp to his belt when Nate returned. The boy showed it off proudly. "I can't wait until I have a whole string," he declared. "Maybe one day I'll have so many I can make a coat out of them like that Mandan we saw once."

Nate squatted in front of his son, tapped the scalp, and said softly, "That there was part of a human being, Zach. A living, breathing person like you and me. A person whose life I just took. It must never be taken lightly." He fingered the silken strands. "Think of how many lives you would have to take to make a whole coat."

"A heap," Zach said thoughtfully.

"I know the Shoshones and other tribes see it differently, but I can't help thinking that the Good Lord didn't put us here to spend our days wiping each other out. There has to be more to life than killing."

"I see your point, Pa. I'm sorry I got carried away."

Nate tousled his son's hair and grinned. "You had it wrong before. You don't have the best father. I have the best son." He gave the boy a firm hug, and as he did he saw Long Holy giving them both a peculiar look.

"What do we do next, Grizzly Killer?" the Shoshone asked, but a bit too quickly, as if he was bothered at being caught.

"We haul these bodies off, cover them with brush, and hide somewhere," Nate answered, standing. "The rest of the Utes are bound to come searching for their friends, and we do not want to be here when they do."

"I will take care of the bodies," Long Holy offered. Going to the one he had lanced, he gripped the man by the ankles and began dragging him away.

Nate walked to Winona, who was untying her mare, and looping his arms around her slender waist, kissed her on the ear.

"What was that for, husband?"

"For being the most contrary female this side of the Divide."

"I must remember to be contrary more often."

"What you did was very brave," Nate said, stepping to the stallion, "but you took too big a chance. What if those Utes had put an arrow or a lance into you the moment they laid eyes on you?"

"Into a lone woman with a baby at her breast?" Winona laughed. "I think not, dearest. They were too curious to kill me, as any man would have been."

"Not all men. There are some who kill others for the thrill of it."

Winona stared at him, then came to his side. Holding Evelyn out of the way, she made sure Long Holy was nowhere in sight before kissing Nate full on the lips. "Your concern is touching. We can argue about this another day, if you wish. For now, all that matters is the trick worked and we are still alive."

"Just don't ever pull a stunt like that again. If the hostiles don't get us, I may just naturally keel over when my heart gives out."

Once Long Holy had attended to the corpses, Nate and the warrior scattered leaves and pines needles about to cover their tracks and the blood. Only when Nate was satisfied a casual glance would not arouse suspicion did he mount up and head back through the stand to a boulder-strewn hill situated a mile from the stream.

Having tied the horses on the opposite side, Nate hiked to the top and took a seat on a flat boulder commanding an excellent view of the entire valley. His family and Long Holy followed his example.

"Once the sun sets," Nate announced, "I'm paying those Utes a visit. If I can get the drop on them, I can take them all prisoner."

"You will surround all ten of them by yourself?" Winona said. "Utes are not Otoes. They will not line up meekly simply because you cover them with a gun.

As soon as you show yourself, they will be on you like a pack of wolves." She shook her head. "Zach and I must come with you."

"Not on your life," Nate said, refusing to concede this time. He glanced at the warrior, half-expecting Long Holy to offer to help, but the brave was gazing rather longingly toward the mouth of the valley. Why? Nate mused. What was behind the warrior's increasingly strange behavior?

Zach had heard his mother and leaped right in. "I can lend a hand, Pa. I'm big enough now to know what I'm doing."

"No."

"But how am I supposed to learn how to be a warrior if you won't let me do the things warriors do?"

"Don't push it, son. I'm not—" Nate began, and completely forgot the rest of what he was about to say when a savage snarl erupted at the base of the hill and the horses went into a frenzy of fear. Shoving up, he dashed to the side, and was stupefied to see a young panther in the act of stalking the mare. Body low to the ground, tail flicking wildly, the big cat glided through the grass as if walking on air.

Nate raised the Hawken, then remembered the Utes. The sound of a shot might carry that far. So waving the rifle overhead and bellowing like an angry bull, he raced down the slope.

The panther spun, hissed, and stubbornly held its ground until Nate was nearly to the bottom. In a blur it was off, bounding ten feet at a stride, to vanish in the evergreens.

Nor was it alone. At the very moment the cat fled, so did Winona's mare, in the other direction. The reins slipped off the low limb to which Winona had fastened them, and fearing for its life even though the panther was leaving, the horse sped southward, heading up the valley, heading toward the Utes.

"Damn it all! Can't nothing go right anymore?" Nate muttered, running to the stallion. He had to stop the mare before the Utes spotted her. Mounting, he yelled, "Stay here until I get back!" and galloped on her heels.

Endowed with exceptional strength and speed, the mare had already covered close to 50 yards. Mane flowing, nostrils and eyes wide, she was rivaling the wind.

Nate knew the signs. The mare was so panic-stricken, she'd go for miles if not stopped, running until she was too tired to run another step. And if the Utes saw her, the fur would fly, as the trappers liked to say.

Unfortunately for Nate, wanting to catch the mare was a far cry from actually doing so. Despite the stallion's best efforts, she was more than holding her own. Over long distances she was no match for the black, but over short stretches she was a regular hellion.

Nate cursed passionately when the mare broke from the trees and took to the open ground. Every foot she went now brought her that much closer to certain discovery by the Utes. He almost wished she would step into a prairie-dog hole and go down, busted leg or no. Keeping one eye on the column of smoke, he lashed the stallion furiously and rode, rode, rode.

Presently the mare showed signs of flagging. Nate gained swiftly, leaning far out so he could snatch her bridle when he was near enough. Not 30 seconds later he was, and with a cry of elation he brought the mare to a pounding stop.

Overjoyed, Nate seized her reins, and was turning the stallion when he saw four warriors by the trees, all studies in consternation. Two bore armloads of wood for their fire, which they dropped at a word from one of their companions, and all four charged toward him, venting awful shrieks and whoops.

Nate didn't dare go back to the hill; he'd lead the Utes right to his loved ones. Bearing eastward, he pushed the stallion to its limits, knowing full well there would be mounted Utes in pursuit at any second. He was closing on a tract of brush when his deduction was borne out.

Five Utes on horseback exploded from the trees, soon passing their fellows on foot.

Now Nate was in serious trouble. He crashed into the brush and altered course to the north, then the east again, using the maze of thickets to the best advantage. In a haphazard pattern he put hundreds of yards behind him. At length the brush ended at the rim of a gully, down which he shot at breakneck speed. On the bottom he turned to the right and gave the stallion its head. The tired mare resisted but Nate jerked on the reins, forcing her to keep up.

Several minutes had gone by, and Nate had left the gully for sheltering forest when it occurred to him that he should have seen some sign of the Utes by then. Stopping, he listened, and was disturbed to hear nothing but the wind where there should have been harsh yells and the drum of many hoofs.

What were the devils up to? Nate wondered. Evidently they were not even trying to stick to his trail. Why not? Had they fanned out instead? Was one of them already close enough to put an arrow into him?

Simultaneous with the thought, Nate saw a warrior materialize off to the left. They both spotted each other at the same time. The Ute lifted a bow. Nate snapped up the Hawken. By the merest fraction his rifle blasted first and the Ute pitched rearward, the arrow zipping into the earth.

"My fat's in the fire!" Nate declared, making off to the south. The shot would draw every last Ute to the scene and they would be on him in no time. No matter,

Nate had to stop and reload, which he did when he came on a wide hollow.

The proper amount of black powder had been poured into the barrel, and Nate was in the act of shoving the ball and patch down with the ramrod, when the crunch of something large moving through the underbrush rimming the hollow caused him to pause. Twisting, he saw the outline of a horse and rider, a Ute and a war-horse. The brave was gazing off in the distance, apparently seeking him.

Nate held his breath until the Ute had gone. Quickly he finished loading, inserted the ramrod into its housing, and headed for the shallow end of the hollow to leave. More crunching stopped him cold.

Three or four Utes were to the west, moving abreast. Nate ducked low over the saddle, relying on the rim to shield him. When the clump of hoofs died in the distance he straightened, jabbed his heels into the stallion's flanks, and took the incline on the fly.

Nate had been doing such a fine job of losing the Utes that now he was disoriented himself. The hill, by his reckoning, should be to the north. Or was it the northeast? Since the war party had gone to the south, his options were the east and the west. Bearing west, however, would take him to the stream and open space. So eastward was his best bet.

Reins firmly clasped, the Hawken slanted across his thighs, Nate wound deeper into the trees. He intended to go a few miles, then when he was certain he had lost the Utes, swing around toward the hill. At the rate he was going, it would be well after dark before he was reunited with Winona and the others, and he hoped Winona didn't become impatient and come looking for him. She might stumble on Utes herself.

Preoccupied with worry about his family, Nate skirted a rocky spine that appeared out of nowhere. He had gone a few dozen feet along its base when a twig snapped above him. Glancing up, he was shocked to behold a Ute at the very instant the warrior pounced.

Nate tried to bring the Hawken up, but he only had the rifle to chest height when the brave smashed into him, flinging him from the stallion. He felt the Hawken leave his fingers before his back smacked down with so much force every bone in his body was jarred and the breath whooshed from his lungs.

In moments of extreme stress the human body is capable of extraordinary feats. When imperiled, a person can move faster, react faster, attack faster. So it was with Nate King as he saw the Ute lift a tomahawk on high to bury the blade in his torso. Like lightning he rolled to the right, the thud of the weapon telling him how close he had come to giving up the ghost.

Flipping back again, Nate drove his right foot into the Ute's knee. There was a loud crack. Grimacing, the Ute swung the tomahawk, but this time Nate met it with his own. The blow rocked his shoulder.

Nate scrambled out of reach and pushed to his feet. The Ute came at him, limping but not out of the fight, features fixed in vicious determination. Nate ducked under a swipe that would have decapitated him, and retaliated by trying to take the Ute's arm off at the elbow. He missed, leaving himself wide open. The Ute lunged, aiming at Nate's throat. By whipping rearward Nate evaded the tomahawk.

Now they circled one another, seeking a weakness that could be exploited.

Suddenly the Ute tilted his head and voiced a piercing series of yips.

The meaning was obvious. Other warriors would hear and respond, and Nate would find himself hopelessly outnumbered. Nate had to end the fight, end it hastily, or suffer the consequences. With that goal in mind he shifted and swung, deliberately aiming a few inches wide to the right to drive the Ute to the left. His tactic worked, and as the Ute raised his tomahawk to deflect another attack, Nate stepped in close, on the left, and streaked his butcher knife from its sheath on his left hip into the Ute's chest.

Not a single sound escaped the Ute's lips. He staggered, gawked at the hilt, then toppled.

Not having a second to waste, Nate ripped the knife out, replaced it, slipped the tomahawk under his belt, and reclaimed the Hawken. The stallion and the mare had only gone a dozen yards, so in short order he was mounted and about to depart. Then he saw the Ute's war-horse.

The animal stood atop the spine, reins dangling, patiently awaiting its lord and master.

To the south arose shouts and yips, signifying the rest of the band was on its way.

"Heeeeyah!" Nate said, urging the stallion upward. He was afraid the war-horse would run off but it stayed put, allowing him to stop, lift its reins, and cuff it on the rump. It bolted into the woods to the west, making enough noise for ten animals as it plowed through the brush. Nate continued eastward, grinning as he listened to the war party, which had changed direction and was now chasing the slain brave's mount.

Good riddance, Nate reflected, although he knew they would be hotter than ever for his scalp once they realized they had been duped. The next ten minutes were spent galloping over hill and down dale in an effort to gain a wide lead. His flight brought him to the lower slope of a lofty mountain. By then the mare was so fatigued she was balking.

Nate decided to get higher, to attain a point where he could survey the surrounding countryside and see the Utes coming long before they saw him. A ravine afforded him the means of doing so without being spotted from below. Where a section of wall had buckled, Nate goaded his horses up onto a flat shelf carpeted with grass. Here he dismounted, ground-hitched both animals, and crept to the edge.

From so high up the valley was deceptively peaceful but undeniably lovely, with the blue stream like a colorful ribbon wrapped around a bright green package.

Lying down so he could prop his chin in his hands, Nate scoured the forest for his adversaries. He was confident he had eluded them, and concentrated on the vegetation to the west, where the fleeing horse would have lured them. Hunt as he might, he failed to see a single brave.

Nate was inclining to the opinion the Utes had given up and returned to their camp when his gaze strayed to the base of the mountain on which he roosted. Shock brought an oath from his lips.

Lined up in a row facing the slope were ten Utes, and each and every one was staring directly at the shelf—directly at Nate.

Chapter Twelve

The Rattler hefted his lance and declared gruffly, "If my own eyes had not seen him, I would not believe it! How can he be here when he should be back in the village of Mighty Thunder in Sky being put to death? Something has gone terribly wrong, and I do not know what it is."

"Why are you upset?" Leaping Wolf asked.

"Did you not recognize the white dog? It is Grizzly Killer himself."

"How can you be sure?" Leaping Wolf asked. "With all that hair they grow, all whites look alike to me." He snickered. "Their faces remind me of the hind ends of bears. Only the bears are better-looking."

Laughter greeted the insult. Holds the Arrows waved his bow and said, "Does it matter who this white man is? Let us count coup on him so our people will be even more impressed by the success of our raid."

"Do not be so impetuous," The Rattler declared. "He is mine. I claim the right to strike him down."

"Why you?" one of the others demanded.

"Because twice I had it in my power to slay him and could not. Because somehow he has ruined my plan. And because I have promised myself that his hair belongs in my lodge, and mine alone."

"Those are not reasons," the dissenter said. "Each of us has as much right as you do to take his scalp."

"Do you?" The Rattler hissed. "If those were not good enough for you, perhaps this reason will be better." He slapped his quirt against the side of his horse and in a twinkling was upon the startled warrior. Before the man could defend himself, the two horses collided and the dissenter's was sent tumbling. Had the warrior not thrown himself out from under the falling animal, he would have been pinned.

The Rattler whooped with glee and raked the rest with a hawkish stare. "Who else thinks I do not have the right to slay Grizzly Killer?"

None of the others spoke, although several shifted uneasily.

"As I thought," The Rattler said. He jabbed his lance skyward. "If I have not come back by the time the sun is straight overhead, feel free to kill the white bastard yourselves."

"Can I go with you, Uncle?" Holds the Arrows requested.

The Rattler was on the verge of refusing when he thought of how he might benefit. "Very well. But you are to stay back, observe, and learn. And when we reach our village, you can tell all of our people how you saw me kill the great Grizzly Killer. As the only witness, you will be one of the most sought-after men in the village."

"You honor me," Holds the Arrows said, and could not understand why Leaping Wolf had a fit of coughing.

"Come," The Rattler directed. "My lance thirsts for white blood!"

Nate saw the warrior with the nasty disposition and the young one break away from the band and gallop into the ravine he had used in his ascent. He watched the others for a few seconds, figuring they would come at him from another direction, but all they did was move their mounts closer together and begin an animated conversation.

Drawing back, Nate rose and ran to the top of the collapsed section. He could see for over a hundred yards, to a bend. Confident picking the Utes off before they reached him would be child's play, he took cover next to a shoulder-high boulder and aligned the Hawken on top.

Minutes dragged by with excruciating slowness. Nate shifted from foot to foot and nervously wrung his hands. By his calculations the pair should appear at any time, yet they didn't. Puzzled, he moved to another boulder, one a score of feet closer to the bend.

They were up to something. That was Nate's conclusion after five more minutes passed without incident. Cocking the Hawken, he advanced to the rim. Boulders littered the bottom of the ravine but nothing moved among them, not even chipmunks. A span of only 30 feet separated him from the other side, well within the range of a skilled archer, but there were no places for a man to conceal himself; it was bare of plant growth and boulders.

Nate pondered whether he should try to escape up the mountain. The slopes were steep, but not so steep the stallion and mare couldn't make it to the top. Getting down the other side before the Utes came around might pose some difficulty, leaving him no better off than he was right there.

Disgusted for having boxed himself in, Nate turned away from the rim, and as he moved an arrow zipped past his cheek so close to his skin he felt the feathers tickle his flesh. Instantly he dove behind a boulder.

No more shafts were fired. His head flush with the ground, Nate crawled to a different boulder. He knew the young warrior had shot at him because only the young one had a bow. The nasty Ute had carried a lance.

So where was the bowman? Nate asked himself. If not at the bottom or on the other rim, then where? He tried to remember which direction the arrow had come from and couldn't.

The black stallion suddenly nickered.

Nate looked and saw the horse gazing across the ravine. Poking his head out, he sought in vain for the young Ute. It reminded him of the time he had fought Apaches, masters at camouflaging themselves in any type of terrain, at seemingly turning invisible right before a person's eyes. A man could be staring right at one and not even realize it.

Utes were good, but they were not quite that good. Nate searched and searched, and so intent was he on locating the archer that he nearly missed hearing the whisper of falling dirt at the front of the shelf.

Rising into a crouch, Nate dashed to the edge and warily took a peek. There was a sheer drop-off of eight or nine feet from the top of the shelf to the slope below, and trying to climb it was the young warrior. The brave had scaled five feet but was stranded, unable to get a firm enough purchase with both hands to pull himself higher because he was carrying a lance in his right.

The two of them had exchanged weapons, Nate realized. Why he had no idea, nor did it matter. He grabbed a pistol and leaned out to shoot as warning shouts from the band below alerted the young warrior to his plight.

Looking up, the brave saw Nate and jerked backwards in fright, which caused him to lose not only his grip on the drop-off but on the lance as well. He fell, tumbling end over end once he struck the slope, unable to arrest his fall until he had gone over 20 feet. No sooner did he come to a stop than he frantically dived behind a boulder.

Nate held his fire. He wasn't about to shoot unless he was certain of hitting his target. And too, he was disinclined to kill an unarmed man.

Suddenly Nate remembered the vicious warrior with the bow. He whirled, hoping he hadn't stupidly exposed himself. But he had. Standing on the far rim, taking aim, his face lit by a peculiar smile, was the other warrior.

The Rattler was smiling because he was about to make a kill, and because his ploy had worked so perfectly. Holds the Arrows had been flattered when The Rattler asked to trade weapons, and had been eager to distract Grizzly Killer so The Rattler could strike. The inexperienced fool hadn't appreciated the risk he was taking. A lance was no match for a rifle or a pistol, as The Rattler was keenly aware. A bow, though, was the equal of a rifle any day.

Of course the white dog had fallen for the trick. Prone in a crack in the ground produced by some ancient upheaval, The Rattler had watched Grizzly Killer, and waited until the trapper was peering over the edge of the shelf before rising and drawing back the bowstring. He had sighted along the shaft, going for a heart shot, when Grizzly Killer had unexpectedly whirled.

Now The Rattler shifted the bow a few inches to compensate, took a fraction of time to steady the shaft, and let his fingers go slack. The arrow flew almost swifter than the eye could follow. As it did, The Rattler widened his smile in anticipation of seeing Grizzly Killer transfixed. Instead, he saw the trapper twist at the very last moment, saw the arrow point crease the white man's buckskin shirt but spare the flesh underneath, and The

Rattler's smile changed into a howl of rage.

Then The Rattler saw Grizzly Killer raise a pistol. Spinning, he flattened just as the gun roared, and he heard the ball go by. He snaked into the crack, and kept on crawling until he was hidden by an earthen mound over 30 yards from the ravine. A cautious glance showed no trace of his hated enemy.

Supreme frustration made The Rattler clench his fists until his knuckles turned white. He had missed! And no doubt Leaping Wolf and the others were having a fine laugh at his expense. The only way he could redeem himself was by taking Grizzly Killer's scalp.

How to go about it was the big question. The Rattler could not get anywhere near the rim except by means of the crack, and since the trapper must be expecting him to do just that, he'd be shot the instant he popped up. Nor was he about to go all the way back down the mountain so he could cross to the other side of the ravine and try to sneak within bow range from below. No, there had to be another way, and an examination of the slope *above* the shelf suggested one to him.

His stomach scraping the ground, The Rattler worked ever farther from the ravine. When he felt safe, he stood and picked his way higher, staying out of sight of the shelf. Once he paused to look, but saw only a stallion and a mare.

The sun was steadily climbing too. The Rattler remembered telling the others they could attack once it was directly overhead, and he wanted to pound a rock against his head for being so witless. Now he must hurry or Leaping Wolf and the rest might steal the glory from him.

Approximately 50 yards above the shelf, the ravine ended. Pines and abundant brush permitted The Rattler to pass undetected to the other side, and from there to stealthily creep lower and lower until he was perched behind a boulder affording a bird's eye view of the whole shelf. Oddly enough, he saw no trace of Grizzly Killer.

Not five minutes earlier, the Ute would have.

Nate King had been on his stomach, the Hawken extended, impatiently waiting for either the vicious warrior or the young one to reappear. When time went on and neither did, it occurred to Nate that he was virtually asking to be killed by remaining there and doing nothing. Rather than let them carry the fight to him, he should take the initiative and turn the tables by becoming the aggressor.

Moving to the opposite end of the shelf from the ravine, Nate climbed higher through a maze of boulders and stunted trees. He had gone less than ten yards when he spotted movement, and shortly thereafter he saw the mean-looking Ute, the one who had rammed his horse into another brave's mount, gliding toward the shelf.

Nate fixed a bead on the warrior's head, and was about to cock the hammer when an idea hit him. He needed one of the Utes alive to take back to Mighty Thunder in Sky so the chief could unravel the truth about the death of Dog with Horns. Since to Nate's utter surprise the rest of the war party was still down at the base of the mountain, making no attempt to kill him, and since the young brave was somewhere below and not likely to intervene, Nate knew he might never have a more ideal opportunity to take one of the Utes alive.

So as the warrior was taking up a position in the shadow of a boulder, Nate was bearing down on him with the skill of a stalking lynx. He deposited the Hawken in a patch of grass, drew his tomahawk, and flitted from cover to cover until he was above the warrior and slightly to the right.

Nate coiled his legs for his leap. A glancing blow should suffice to render the brave unconscious; then Nate would cut strips from the Ute's buckskins to bind him.

The Rattler, meanwhile, was scouring every nook and cranny in an effort to locate the one man he detested more than any other. That Grizzly Killer had been able to resist the efforts of the Utes to drive him from the mountains was a source of deep anger and embarrassment. The Rattler took great pride in being a Ute, in being a noted member of a powerful tribe able to hold its own against the Comanches and the Blackfeet. Yet this lone white man stood firm against them!

Abruptly, something seemed to blot out the sunlight, and The Rattler twisted to see Grizzly Killer swooping down upon him like a mighty bird of prey. The Rattler had the bow and an arrow in his hands, but loosing the shaft before the trapper was on him would be impossible. He could do no more than hurl both at his foe while springing backward and clawing at his knife.

Nate barely felt the sting of the bow and arrow when they hit his chest, so intent was he on bringing the warrior down. He clipped the Ute on the shoulder, which sent the man flying, and smacked down beside the boulder.

The Rattler recovered quickly, his knife a blur as he took a stride and thrust.

In the act of rising, Nate parried the sweeping blade with his tomahawk, reversed direction, and drove the tomahawk at the Ute's leg.

Had The Rattler been a shade slower, he would have been crippled. By a hair he yanked his leg from the path of his enemy's weapon, then countered by spearing his knife at Grizzly Killer's neck.

Nate blocked the swing, skipped to one side, and tried to slam the flat of his tomahawk into the warrior's temple. The brave ducked, pivoted, struck. Sparks flew as the steel blade scraped the head of the tomahawk.

The Rattler moved in, weaving a glittering web of flashing light as he tried to pierce the white man's guard and deliver a fatal stab.

Nate was hard pressed to keep the knife at bay. His tomahawk was heavier, slightly more difficult to wield. He had to keep his arm ceaselessly in motion, countering, deflecting, feinting. Another handicap under which he fought was his resolve to take the brave alive. It would have been so much simpler to kill the Ute outright. Still, he stuck by his decision. Legs rooted, he gave as good as he got for a seeming eternity.

Then The Rattler dropped under a stroke that would have had him seeing stars, and at the lowest point of his crouch he reached down and scooped up a handful of dirt.

Focused on the knife, Nate didn't see the warrior's left hand until it flicked at his face and dirt was tossed at his eyes. He tried to bring his left hand up to protect himself, but wasn't in time. Some of the dirt caught him right where the Ute wanted and suddenly everything was a blur. In desperation Nate backed away at full speed.

The Rattler smirked and charged. He could see tears pouring from the white man's eyes, and knew victory was in his grasp. Whipping the knife on high, he dashed forward. His arm muscles hardened for the final plunge.

"He is mine, Uncle! I claim the coup!"

The Rattler heard the words, but they failed to register for the few heartbeats his brain needed to send an impulse along his nerves to his hand. His knife arced downward, biting deep into yielding tissue. But not the tissue of the trapper. For as The Rattler drove the knife home, another figure hurtled between Grizzly Killer and him, the figure of his simpleton of a nephew, who took the blade squarely between the shoulder blades.

Nate saw the second brave appear, but his vision was so murky because of his watering eyes that he could not quite tell what had happened. He heard the newcomer shout, distinguished the dark outline of a lance, and thinking the newcomer was about to plunge it into him, he darted to the left, ran smack into a boulder, and fell.

The Rattler was too incensed to notice, incensed at his nephew for being such an idiot and at himself for being so trusting. He should have known Holds the Arrows would not be content to stay out of the way while he dispatched Grizzly Killer. Whoever did so would earn glory such as few warriors ever achieved; the coup would be talked about whenever extraordinary deeds of valor were discussed for generations to come. And since warriors craved glory in battle above all else, the temptation had proved too much for Holds the Arrows to resist.

Nate had gotten to one knee and was frenetically blinking and rubbing his eyes in an effort to clear his vision. Although perplexed as to why the two Utes didn't press their advantage, he was grateful for their negligence. A few more seconds and he would be able to defend himself again.

The Rattler stared at the blood oozing from the back of his nephew and grunted in disgust. With an indignant twist of his wrist he wrenched the blade free and gave the body a shove to one side. Then, rotating, he saw the trapper rising. Rabid wrath flooded through him as, uttering an inarticulate roar, he leaped.

At that precise second Nate's tears washed the last of the gritty dirt from his eyes and he could see again. He managed to bring the tomahawk up to keep the knife from tearing into his neck, but the weight of the Ute bore him down. His left hand clamped on the other's knife arm at the wrist even as the warrior seized his right wrist and, locked together, they rolled back and forth, both striving to wrest their arms loose so they could use their weapons.

The Rattler marveled at the white man's strength. Long had he believed that whites were inferior in every respect to Indians. In his estimation all trappers were treacherous, cowardly, and weak, fitting and easy prey, to be disposed of at will. The only reason that Grizzly Killer had withstood his people for so long was because of the whites' devious nature and more luck than any one person deserved. It had never occurred to him that Grizzly Killer might be his equal in man-to-man combat, and finding this to be true was a profound shock.

Nate's shoulder hit a boulder and he winced. So far he was holding his own, but his injured wrist was weakening. The wound caused by the dog had not yet healed, and before long the wrist would give out completely. To prevail he must take drastic action and take it immediately. Suddenly he wound up on his back and the brave bore down even harder. Nate drove both knees up into the Ute's stomach, then straightened his legs at the same time he rolled back on his shoulders. The result was as he intended.

The Rattler sailed over his foe and smashed face-first into the dust with a thud. Though he was dazed, his rage was such that it lent power to his sinews and he pushed to his hands and knees, determined to finish Grizzly Killer off in the next few moments or to perish in the attempt.

Nate beat the Ute off the ground. A single stride brought him next to his adversary. He planted his right foot in the warrior's ribs, drew back his leg again, and kicked the brave on the chin.

Bursts of white light exploded before The Rattler. His senses swam. His arms buckled. He tried to heave erect and couldn't. The trapper came closer, undoubtedly to finish him off, and in despair The Rattler did the only thing he could think of. He tackled the trapper around the ankles.

Just as Nate was raising his tomahawk for the decisive blow, his legs were swept out from under him. He saw the Ute's knife being hoisted, and bent forward to ward off the blow. Anxious to triumph, he then followed through with a punch that rocked The Rattler backwards. But it wasn't enough.

The Rattler refused to go down. He had not worked so strenuously to have it all be for nothing. The long ride from Ute country to Grizzly Killer's lodge, the longer ride at reckless speed to the village of Dog with Horns, and again the trailing of Dog with Horns until a suitable ambush site appeared—all that work must not be in vain. It had taken a lot out of him, but not so much that he was unequal to the occasion. He absorbed the white man's punch, rammed a fist into Grizzly Killer's groin, and prepared to sink his knife into the man's unprotected stomach.

Nate knew he was moments away from death. His groin was aflame with pain, his body battered and bruised. He could barely think, yet he realized his crazy notion to take the Ute alive had proven impossible and unless he switched his strategy fast he was going to leave Winona a widow. So as the Ute went to bury the knife in his gut, Nate drew a pistol, slanted the barrel upward, and fired.

Down at the base of the mountain, a warrior named Otter Foot heard and declared, "The white dog is still alive!"

"Perhaps he has killed The Rattler," suggested Lone Elk.

"Or Holds the Arrows," Leaping Wolf said. He glanced at the sun, which was close to being directly overhead. "It is not yet time, but I do not care. We have waited long enough. If The Rattler has not counted coup on Grizzly Killer yet, it is his own fault." Waving his bow, he whooped several times, then asked, "Who is with me?"

"We all are!" Otter Foot answered, and the rest gave their assent.

In a ragged line the eight braves headed for the ravine.

Nate shoved the Ute off him and wearily stood. He had come as close as he ever had to giving up the ghost, and now he wanted nothing more than to rejoin his family. But as he walked to the Hawken a series of savage yells reminded him he was far from out of danger. Running to the rim, he was bewildered to find the Utes had vanished. A swirling cloud of dust at the mouth of the ravine told him where they had gone.

The moment of truth was at hand. If Nate could hold them off, if he could inflict high enough losses, the rest might see fit to leave him be. Reloading on the fly, he raced to the boulder that overlooked the bend and set all three guns out in front of him.

Echoes of hoofs clattering on rock rolled up the ravine like the sound of distant thunder.

Nate wiped his hands on his leggings and gazed out at the valley floor, wondering if this was the spot where he would finally join the ranks of the hundreds of trappers who had paid the ultimate price for their devotion to personal freedom and happiness. Movement in a clearing narrowed his gaze, and an intake of breath was his reaction to seeing more Utes, 20 warriors or better, galloping toward the mountain.

"This is it, I reckon," Nate said aloud, and wistfully looked at his horses. A mad dash down the ravine seemed preferable to dying trapped on the shelf, but before he could do so the eight Utes surged into sight.

Tucking the Hawken to his shoulder, Nate sighted on

the foremost rider, a lean brave carrying a bow. He steadied the rifle, mentally ticked off a three-count, and fired. The lead rider went down, to be trampled by some of the others.

Nate grabbed both pistols, sprinted to the edge, and aimed. The Utes had spotted him. They were trying to scatter, but in the confines of the ravine there was nowhere to go. His first shot dropped a warrior sporting two feathers. His second shot hit a brave in the shoulder. The man reeled, somehow was able to hold on tight, and began to flee.

So did the others. The folly of attempting a frontal assault having been made clear, they retreated around the bend to regroup.

Nate was cramming powder and lead into his guns. The sound of hoofbeats died, which meant the remaining Utes had dismounted and would come after him on foot. He kept his eyes on the opposite rim and the boulders dotting the bottom.

Minutes went by and Nate saw no one. He figured they were tending to the man he had wounded, which gave him a chance to change position. With both pistols under his belt and the Hawken in hand, Nate edged lower. He stopped when the walls reverberated once more to the drum of hoofs. The reinforcements had arrived, and now the Utes would swarm up after him in force.

Rather abruptly a new element reached Nate's ears, the harsh cries and bloodthirsty yips of warriors in battle. On and on it lasted. Confused, he saw a single Ute run around the bend, and brought the rifle to bear. But the Ute had not gone more than a few yards when he fell, revealing an arrow stuck in his back.

Then a warrior on horseback appeared, a powerful figure astride a magnificent war-horse the likes of which few braves ever owned. Wearing a smile, this warrior advanced until he was at the base of the wall on which

Nate stood. "My heart is glad at finding you alive, Grizzly Killer."

Nate was too astounded to do other than blurt out, "Mighty Thunder in Sky! What are you doing here?"

"Making sure you were not killed. You are too valuable a friend to the Shoshones to risk losing you."

"But how—?" Nate said.

"How did we find you?" The chief laughed. "By following the signs Long Holy left for us. Do you remember the day you fled from our village? I told him to take the fastest horse, go on ahead, and see if you would let him join you. We did not want you facing those who slew my brother alone."

"You didn't think I was to blame?"

Mighty Thunder in Sky straightened. "The Shoshones are not in the habit of making fools chiefs. From all that I had heard about you in the past from Broken Paw, Touch the Clouds, and others, I knew you were an honorable man. I also knew how proud you are to be an adopted Shoshone. So I could not accept that you had been a party to the ambush."

"But the parfleche and my horse?"

"Another thing I have heard about you is that you are brother to the fox. Would such a man be so stupid as to leave such things behind?"

Nate had to lean against a boulder. The surprising revelations were coming so fast and furious he could hardly believe what he was hearing. "You were counting on me to find the ones who did it? You expected me to succeed where Standing Bull and the others had failed?"

"Let us say I had great hope. You were taught by Wolverine himself, and he is the best tracker who has ever lived." Mighty Thunder in Sky paused. "So I let you go on without interference, but stayed close enough to be on hand if you needed me."

"It would have been easier for you to catch up and explain."

"And have you shoot one of us before we made our intentions known? Or have those who were not convinced of your innocence, like Standing Bull, try to slay you? No, it was better to let you go your own way until the proper moment."

As the full import of the chief's disclosure impressed themselves on Nate's mind, he chuckled and said, "I compliment your wisdom, but you are wrong about one thing."

"I am?"

"There is a fox here, my friend, but it is not me."

Epilogue

From high out of the sparkling blue sky flew a large golden eagle, its pinions spread as it glided across a verdant secluded valley. Below appeared many of the strange nests it had seen before, the nests of buffalo hide favored by the bizarre two-legged creatures.

The eagle was upset by the size and sounds of the gathering. There were hundreds and hundreds of nests, and among them moved countless numbers of the noisy beings, many chanting and singing and yelling with gleeful abandon. They were too loud, so loud it grated on the eagle, louder than the mighty bird had ever heard before, as if they were caught up in a great celebration of life.

At the center of the gathering sat a large circle of such creatures passing around a branch from which smoke wafted when they puffed on one end. The eagle checked its glide to make a pass over them, its keen eyes noting that one of the creatures appeared to be of a slightly different kind from the rest in that its face was covered with hair while the rest had bare faces.

As the eagle watched, two creatures crowned with many feathers of its own kind approached the hairy one and offered an object that glittered in the sunlight. At this all the creatures let out a mighty yell, which bothered the eagle so much that it banked high into the crisp mountain air and soared off to find the tranquility it craved.

THE BIG FIFTY

JOHNNY D. BOGGS

Young Coady McIlvain spends his days reading about the heroic exploits of the legendary heroes of the West, especially the glorious Buffalo Bill Cody. The harsh reality of frontier life in Kansas becomes brutally clear to Coady, however, when his father is scalped and he is taken prisoner by Comanches. When he is finally able to escape, Coady finds himself with a buffalo sharpshooter who he imagines is the living embodiment of his hero, Buffalo Bill. But real life is seldom like a dime novel, and Fate has more hard lessons in store for Coady—if he can stay alive to learn them.

PETER DAWSON

GHOST BRAND OF THE WISHBONES

Peter Dawson's fiction has retained its classic status among readers of many generations. This volume presents for the first time in paperback three of his most enduring short novels. The title tale opens with the daring robbery of an entire cattle train and gets only more exciting from there. "Hell's Half Acre" is filled with the chaos and danger that results from an all-out range war between cattle ranchers and the sheep raising syndicate. And in "Sagerock Sheriff," old Tom Platt faces his toughest challenge since he took office years ago. He has to find out—right away—if a man being sentenced to life in the penitentiary is really guilty of murder.